GABRIELLE MARIE KOZAK

The Trooper Companions:

The Untold Tales

Contents

Book One: A Violet Blossom

Bakersfield, California.
19 September 2013 A.D.
City Park.

"Throw it to me, Flynn!" the mother urged, her arms held out expectantly. "Come on, you can't have forgotten how to throw, can you?"

Giggling, her four-year-old little girl made a supreme effort at tossing the large, multicolored beach ball. It flew a few feet and then dropped drastically, and would have fallen to the ground had not the nimble woman darted forward and caught it. She panted for effect, making her little girl dissolve into peals of laughter.

"Throw it to me, Mom," the young girl's older sister urged excitedly. She was about seven years old, and her hair was a darker brown than Flynn's, but her eyes were a striking purple. Reaching out, she easily caught the ball when her mother tossed it to her, and bounced it once or twice, grinning. Flynn howled in protest.

"Go on, throw it to her, Grace," the mother told her, struggling to hide a smile. "Good, there you go."

The ball sailed accurately back to Flynn, who made another valiant attempt to send it to her mother, but this time the ball hit the ground and bounced away. Squealing, Flynn ran after it, but the girls' mother had been distracted by an approaching man about her age, who now came within a few meters of the group and stopped.

"Hi, Dad," Grace greeted him, frowning as she walked over to the ball and picked it up. "Do we have to go already?"

Her father gestured towards the sky, smiling at his wife. "Didn't you see the clouds, Grace? It's going to storm soon, and besides, Jason is probably getting hungry by now."

"Jason is such a baby," Flynn declared, scrunching up her face. "Can't Miss Peterson give him his bottle?"

"She probably can, but don't you remember that we were going to give him his first food today?" her father laughed, holding out his hand for her to take. "And besides, you don't want to get all wet when it starts raining, do you?"

With a rebellious glare, Flynn ran over to her mother, taking her hand instead. Laughing, the woman gave her other, free hand to her husband. Grace slipped up to her father and walked beside him, holding the ball under her arm. Together the four made their way out of the city park, heading towards a small minivan. The girls' father—a tall, dark-headed man with gray eyes and accompanying glasses—glanced down at the little girl walking at his side and smiled at the trusting light in her purple eyes.

"Where's Petyr, Steve?" his wife inquired, and Steven Foley tipped his head in the direction of the minivan, where their son was waiting for them.

"He insisted on going on ahead. Can't you see him, Tiana?" Steven's fond smile grew bigger. "He's taller every month."

"We ought to come home more often," Tiana Foley murmured, frowning slightly as a wistful look came into her light green eyes. "Sometimes I'm afraid the children will grow up before we know them."

Steven squeezed her hand reassuringly. "Only a few more months, and we can come back home for a good long while, remember? We just have to get the serum finished. And here we are, not a moment too soon," he added as a crack of thunder rumbled in the air, and Flynn stiffened.

Letting go of his wife's hand, Mr. Foley went around the vehicle quickly and getting into the driver's seat. Grace, and the waiting Petyr scrambled into the back seat of the minivan, and Mrs. Foley buckled Flynn into her car seat. She was just stepping down through the side door to slip into the passenger seat, when the four-year-old protested.

"Mommy, I want you to sit next to me," she yelled pathetically while her two older siblings chortled in the back seat.

After a moment's hesitation, Tiana shrugged, laughing. "Might as well," she admitted, stepping back in and slamming the door shut behind her. It took her only a couple of seconds to sit down and buckle her seat belt.

"Roll call," Steven Foley shouted, having started the car engine.

"Grace here, I have my seat belt on," the eldest replied. This was routine, and she was used to it.

"Petyr here, I have my seat belt on!" her younger brother chimed in.

There was no reaction from the distracted Flynn, who sat staring into space, until her father coughed loudly and her mother nudged her. "Oh, Flynn has her seat belt on!" the four-year-old put in quickly, then glanced at her mother with a proud, satisfied smile.

Steven Foley paused with his hand on the controls for a moment, and called out in affected anxiety, "Where's Jason?"

"He's not here, silly Dad!" Petyr laughed himself to tears, while his father chuckled to himself and started driving.

And so began the fifteen-minute drive to the Foleys' home, with the parents and the two younger children engaging in avid conversation. But the eldest, Grace, didn't typically engage in light chatter, and as the first drops of rain started splattering on the windows, she had her nose pressed up firmly against the glass as she stared out at the gathering storm. As the clouds grew, the eerie light outside found itself reflected in her eyes, and eventually she smiled, a beautiful smile. It was only too obvious that she loved storms.

"It's pouring. Did you bring the umbrella, Tiana?" Steven asked, glancing around the front of the car anxiously.

"Oh, I thought I did...but I can't find it," Tiana sighed, passing up the bag they'd brought for lunch. "Take this in, will you? I'll bring Flynn."

"Okay. Run for it, kids," Steven called back before abruptly throwing his car door open and dashing through the rain to the house.

Quickly, Tiana wrapped her arms around Flynn and made her own escape through the rain. Grace and Petyr followed, Grace being careful to slam the car door shut behind her and her younger brother. Standing on the mat, the seven-year-old took off her wet jacket carefully and hung it on her hook, shivering slightly. It was already starting to be chilly when it rained, being September.

She found her parents and siblings in the kitchen, where Tiana Foley was helping Flynn to dry off and Steven was taking the six-month-old Jason from the family's babysitter.

"Thanks for looking after him, Kayla," Steven smiled. "It was kind of you to let us spend a day with the older three. Especially when you must be looking forward to your vacation."

"It was no trouble at all," Kayla Peterson returned, smiling back. Tall, with light gray eyes and straight brown hair, Kayla was about twenty-two and had only started babysitting for the Foleys two months before.

It should be noted that Mr. and Mrs. Foley were at work in another city three weeks out of every month's four, and so their "babysitter" was actually a full-time nanny for those weeks, taking care of the four children in their parents' absence. The parents were scientists, and worked at a laboratory in a huge, busy city, and they didn't want the children growing up in that kind of dangerous atmosphere. But they made a point of being home as often as they could, and did meeting calls every evening they weren't. They were determined to be good parents, hard as it might be for experienced, talented scientists like them.

Now Tiana was going through the lunch bag, and suddenly she stopped short, sighing. "Look at this, Steve. We had the umbrella with us the entire time."

Glancing in her direction, Steven laughed amusedly. "Well, next time let's look in there, shall we?"

"Definitely," Tiana muttered, sliding an unfinished container of food into the fridge. She looked up suddenly, as if remembering something. "Kayla, are you going home now?"

"I think so," the quiet babysitter returned slowly. "Do you need me?"

"No, I don't think so. Oh, and Kayla—Steve and I will manage everything this week," Tiana added, glancing at the calendar. "You needn't come back until next Sunday, is that okay?"

"Sounds great!" The young woman shifted, picking up her purse from the counter. "Call me if you need anything, Mrs. Foley!"

"Have a great time!" Tiana beamed.

After a few hectic moments in which the three older kids gave their beloved babysitter parting hugs, and baby Jason affected a farewell howl, Kayla finally made her exit. The three children darted back into the kitchen, where their mother was now slicing a banana. Jason was still howling—or he was until his father swung him up, grinning at him, and proceeded to put on an act for the child that would have made any outsider adult immediately write him off as a mental case.

"Can I feed him first? Can I feed him first?" Flynn demanded of her mother, bouncing energetically at her side, and Petyr soon took up the cry as well. Laughing, Tiana glanced around, noticing Grace leaning against the wall by the door, watching her with just a hint of lonesomeness in her purple eyes.

"Grace will give him his first banana slice," Tiana decided, and both the middle children squealed in disbelief.

"That's not fair!" Flynn sulked.

"But then he'll like Grace better than me!" Petyr protested disgustedly.

Their mother laughed at them both. "Don't you realize he's going to spit it out at first?"

* * *

Later that evening, dinner having been eaten and the baby put to bed, the family were gathered in the living room. Petyr had begun to learn to read, and now his mother helped him practice, reading a children's book with him. Grace was quietly finishing her homework, sitting on a corner of the same sofa. Steven was making a brave attempt to get Flynn tired enough for bed—tossing her in the air, a method which the little girl herself strongly recommended, though her mother did not. As the happy whooping continued, Grace furrowed her brows, in an obvious effort to concentrate on her schoolwork. Petyr gave up reading altogether. Mrs. Foley was about to protest when Steven's phone suddenly started ringing from the kitchen.

"Hang on!" he warned the four-year-old, swinging her to his shoulders and making for the kitchen.

"More, Daddy!" she squealed, with antics enough to drive an unmarried man mad. But within a few seconds, Steven had reached his phone; he glanced at the caller ID, then quickly lowered the little girl down to the floor, and answered the call while she threw her arms around his legs in a cute, failed attempt to reclaim his attention.

Aware of her presence, especially when she stepped on his toes, Steven gradually made his way back into the living room, while answering the call. His face changed drastically within the first few seconds.

"Hello? Yes, this is Steven." Tiana glanced up, watching her husband's face furrow as he spoke. "Yes, we're at home right now. Yes, we have plans for tomorrow. What?"

For a few moments his face underwent the changes of some overwhelming emotion, but somehow he managed to keep his voice steady. "No, we can't bring the kids with us! We can't come at all; we're booked out!... An emergency? Why can't Dr. Wilson manage it?"

"Daddy!" Flynn yelled obliviously, dropping the hugging act and devoting her energies to pounding her father's legs with her chubby little fists.

Steven ignored her, and finally her mother called her away, and the little girl ran to Tiana, burying her face in her mother's skirts. Petyr only pulled faces at her.

Meanwhile, Steven's gaze sank to the floor. "Fine, if it's that important. How long do we have? How long will it take? ...I'll have to speak to the kids' babysitter, but I can't make any promises. You'd better make this worth it, Ryan!"

His shoulders slumping in defeat, Steven hung up, slipping his phone into his pocket. He glanced at his wife, and she sighed.

"We're needed back at the lab, aren't we?" she asked softly, running her fingers through Flynn's hair gently.

Steven nodded glumly. "As soon as possible, too. There's been an emergency. An explosion, too, from the sound of it—and Ryan says Laurence is in the hospital. I guess I'd better call Kayla?"

"Guess so," Tiana murmured, and bent down, standing up a moment later with Flynn in her arms. "Come on, Petyr," she added quietly as Steven began dialing a new number.

A few minutes later, after the two's teeth had been brushed and other bedtime preparations had been made, little Flynn had been put to bed, and Tiana crept into the boys' room with Petyr, being acutely aware that Jason was fast asleep in the crib. The two knelt by Petyr's bed, and Tiana folded first Petyr's hands, and then her own. Quickly and quietly she led the prayers and tucked her eldest boy into bed. Her lips brushed his forehead as she kissed him goodnight.

"Sweet dreams, Petyr," she whispered, and straightened, but the five-year-old's fingers wrapped firmly around her arm.

"Mommy, I don't want you and Dad to go. I'm scared," the little boy admitted, looking up at his mother out of wide, frightened eyes.

Tiana affected a small laugh. "What are you scared of, Petyr? I'll leave the light on, and—"

"No, I'm not scared of the dark," Petyr hastened to clarify. His fingers squeezed tighter. "I—I just don't want you to go."

"It's fine, Petyr," Tiana murmured, though her own eyes, green like his, were suddenly moist with unshed tears. "Daddy and I will be back soon, okay? We have to go, but we'll come back and stay for a long time. You'll look after your siblings, won't you?" Tiana asked him quietly, smiling through her tears. "You'll be the man of the house for as long as we're gone, right?"

Her little boy smiled sleepily. "Yeah, I will, Mommy," he assured her, and gradually his grip loosened. It was only a matter of seconds before his hand dropped down onto his chest. He smiled up at Tiana, then closed his eyes.

Tiana stood up and kissed him again. She stepped over to Jason and did the same. After going in to see Flynn, she tiptoed downstairs, brushing the back of her sleeve once across her face in an effort to hide the fact that she had been crying. The sun had long set—it was past nine—and when she went downstairs she was somewhat surprised to see Steven looking through the refrigerator.

"What's up?" she asked him brightly, but when Steven glanced around, he could instantly tell from her eyes that she'd been crying.

"Huh?" he asked, his mind completely blank for a moment.

"Why are you in the fridge?" Tiana iterated patiently.

"Oh, that." Steven shrugged vaguely, sighing. "I checked the flights, and there are none we can get in the next twenty-four hours, so I'm just looking for something we can bring for the drive."

"We're driving, then?" Tiana muttered. "Boy, this had *better* be important."

"I know, right?" Steven mumbled, but at that moment his eyes lit on their eldest as she silently entered the kitchen. "Oh, Grace, why don't you go to bed?"

"I want to go with you," the girl declared suddenly, her purple eyes determined. "Dad, you said you're driving, right? So it wouldn't cost extra for me to go."

"It's not money we're worried about," Steven began, then broke off, his mind seized by a sudden idea. His eyes flew to Tiana's. "Actually, why not?"

Grace gasped in delight, but her mother was startled. "What, Steve, you can't be serious?"

"I am," he admitted sheepishly. "But why can't she come? She can stay at the apartment with us—and Christine can be with her during the day—and—"

"Do you want to go, Grace?" Tiana asked with an air of defeat, though she was secretly delighted at the prospect of her darling little girl accompanying them.

"Mhm," Grace nodded emphatically before remembering her manners. "Please!"

"Well, Steven?" Tiana turned to her husband with an air of finality.

"Yes," he returned, his face breaking into a smile.

It was obvious that Grace would have shouted for excitement, had not her mother just then shushed her. "Let's get ready, Grace," she decided, leading the way out of the room. "We'll need to pack a bag, and you'll have to say goodbye to your siblings. Oh, and you'll have to be very good for Miss Christine Fortner, and..."

While her mother outlined an entire list of restrictions and requirements,

Grace's purple eyes shone in absolute delight as she and her mother quickly went up the stairs and Steven set about contacting Kayla. For the first time since she was a baby, Grace was getting to travel with her parents!

* * *

It was about eleven the next morning, at a hotel in Portland, Oregon, when the hotel doors opened to let in three people: a man, a woman, and a little girl who was obviously their child. All three of them were very tired; indeed, the girl, who was wearing a light yellow jacket, looked as if she had just woken up. She clung tightly to her mother's hand, staring blearily at her surroundings out of drowsy purple eyes.

After identifying himself and his reservation, Steven Foley made no delay in heading for the elevators with his two companions. Once they had all gotten into one, he glanced at his key card, and hit the elevator button to take them to their room's floor. They arrived, not a moment too soon, for Grace was definitely falling asleep again.

Finally they located their room, and lost no time in getting themselves into it and ready for bed. The parents had been driving all night, and every one of the three was exhausted, as they had arrived at the Foley adults' usual accommodations about an hour before, only to discover that that was part of the emergency their confederate had spoken about: the scientists' lodgings had been attacked the evening before, as had the laboratory. But Steven and Tiana were way too exhausted to deal with it now, and the understanding "Ryan" had sent them directly to the hotel, especially as they had brought Grace with them.

The seven-year-old was asleep in seconds, having been tucked into one of the two beds by her equally tired mother. And a few minutes later, the parents were asleep as well, despite the noisy sounds of traffic coming from outside.

They slept soundly, for hours, until Steven's phone rang, at about six in the afternoon. It woke Tiana up first, and then she had to get Steven up, and by the time the phone was answered, Grace was awake as well. She sat on the window seat, staring wonderingly out the window at the city, one story's height below, while her father answered his call.

It was only a couple of seconds before he hung up, angrily slamming his phone down on the bedside table. "Junk," he announced. "Someday I'm going to sue those people. Well, we're up, anyway. What to do now?"

"It's dinner time, isn't it?" Tiana noted, smiling.

"I'm starving," Grace proclaimed, suddenly no longer interested in the view from the window. Rubbing her stomach convincingly, she slipped down from the window seat and stood, waiting expectantly.

Steven laughed. "Well, dinner sounds in order. I'm starving, too," he added pensively. "But I'd just better phone Ryan first, okay?"

* * *

None of the family was aware of the young man sitting on a chair in the hotel corridor, nearly opposite their room door, waiting impatiently. Twice he glanced up and down the hallway as people walked through, then sighed when he saw no one he recognized. It was obvious that he was waiting for someone.

He glanced up again as he heard footsteps, but slouched again with a sigh when he saw it was only one of the hotel employees. He didn't look up when the man walked all the way to the room door across the hallway and knocked.

However, he did look up when the door was opened, and when, instead of quietly stating his concern from outside the door, the employee slipped inside the room, closing the door behind him. The man in the hallway's brow furrowed. Never in his whole life's experience had he noticed a hotel employee actually going inside a room, except to clean it when the occupants weren't inside. He didn't know if the occupants were inside, but it wasn't the cleaning time of the day—and suddenly his first mental question was answered as he faintly heard raised voices from inside the room.

The man's eyebrows shot up, but then he heard a scream—a young girl's terrified scream. He stood up quickly, and froze as two shots, closely following each other, rang out; and then two more.

He was frozen for only an instant before he yelled loudly for help, and dashed over to the door, throwing his hand around the handle. It turned, and he was in. He heard the shattering of glass as the apparent hotel employee threw both his gun and himself out the window. But the man didn't have eyes for him—only for what he left behind him.

There were two casualties, one woman and one man about the same age—both of them dead, as far as he could tell. But neither of them had screamed—he knew as he saw her that it had been the little girl.

She was staring at her parents, her purple eyes dilated in shock and horror. She didn't notice the man—she didn't even seem to be able to cry. She was just frozen still, and for a moment the man wondered if she, too, was dying—but no, she seemed to be physically alright.

Running over, the man placed one hand on her shoulder to steady her, while he fumbled in his pocket with the other hand for his phone, with the obvious intention of calling the police. The girl fell forward, shaking, and he knelt and caught her, gently leaning her against him so she couldn't keep staring at her parents. Quickly he explained the situation to the police, then left his phone on the floor while he held the little girl.

Despite his own state of shocked horror, he was surprised to feel how warm she was. He unzipped her yellow jacket, talking slowly and quietly to her in an attempt to distract both her and himself from the lifeless bodies behind them.

"What's your name? You're going to be alright, little girl, okay?" he assured her, his own hands shaking as the realization of what had happened struck him. "I'm really, really sorry. Be okay, will you? Please? Hey, you've got some beautiful purple eyes, did you know that? Or violet. They're lovely. What's your name, little girl?" He rocked her back and forth in a desperate attempt to elicit some kind of reaction. "My name's Lyndon, did you know that? Lyndon Arnnu. Are you okay? Don't worry, the police will be here soon. And an ambulance or two, probably. I'm so, so sorry. I should have known. I wonder who you are?"

* * *

That was how the police found them, some minutes later. Afterwards, the three family members were rushed to the hospital, while Lyndon Arnnu was asked to come to the police station to answer questions. That changed into identifying the suspect—someone else had reported him while he was running from the scene of the crime. The man refused to talk, even when the head policeman received a call reporting the death of the two parents and announced the fact to the others in the room.

"But who were they?" Lyndon demanded of the officer who led him out, perhaps subconsciously annoyed that no one had told him yet—or maybe it was just an involuntary, natural question. Lyndon gestured helplessly. "Who would do a thing like that?"

"The parents were Mr. and Mrs. Steven Foley, Residents of Bakersfield, California," the policeman informed Lyndon later. "They've been working at a laboratory in this city for years now; their main project is…top secret. Their coworkers' accommodations were attacked last night, as was the laboratory, by members of the same group the perp belongs to. Thank you for your cooperation, Mr. Arnnu," he finished, smiling.

But Lyndon hesitated. "And the little girl? What about her?"

"Oh, their daughter Grace?" The policeman shrugged helplessly. "I hear she is still in an intense state of shock. Probably with amnesia. But she will survive."

"Can I visit her?" Lyndon wondered, but he had to leave his phone number for later. The girl couldn't have any visitors yet, as was perfectly expected only a couple of hours after the incident.

"Grace Foley, huh?" Lyndon murmured to himself as he finally left the police station, hours later. "I think Violet suits her better."

* * *

Over the next few weeks, the affair was gradually cleared up. Lyndon, who came every day to the hospital to visit the little girl, got most of the updates from the nurses, who told him that the three younger Foley children had been placed in the Bakersfield foster care, and that Grace would likely go to join them, once she was judged well enough to leave the medical facility. This decision Lyndon emphatically informed the nurses he was going to attempt to change.

"It's only too clear that she doesn't remember what happened," he pointed out. "Why not let it stay that way, at least for now? She doesn't need to know, does she? And the knowledge will just make her miserable. Someone ought to take her in and give her parents again."

"I'm not the person with whom to discuss that," the nurse returned smoothly. "If you know anyone who would do that for her, why don't you contact the police?"

Lyndon's eyes had lit up with a sudden idea, and he had merely nodded, going in then to see the little girl herself. She was awake, and staring questioningly at Lyndon out of her soft purple eyes. Lyndon had bought her a small stuffed, purple rabbit a few days before, and he was gratified to see that she was holding it. There were other gifts and get-well cards in the room from various other adults who felt sympathy towards the little girl, but Lyndon had inquired and found out that the children had no other close relatives.

He sat down quietly on the chair beside the bed, smiling at the girl. She glanced up at him, and blinked once.

"You're okay, aren't you?" Lyndon asked her quietly. "Say, do you think you'd want to come live with me? I'm not quite out of college yet but I think I could take care of you. How do you like the name Violet?" he continued, talking more to himself than to the girl.

Various thoughts ran through his head as he watched her, and suddenly he felt an indomitable resolve. He had a right—no, a duty—to take care of the little girl, since his own hesitation had possibly destroyed the last hopes of saving her parents. He should have guessed that no real hotel employee would go into the room and close the door. It was his fault, in a way.

But he would make up for it by taking care of little Grace—a little violet, in her own way—though he couldn't afford to take her younger siblings under his wing as well. He would raise her like he would any child of his and protect her from her past, at least for a little while.

He could do that much for her. He could give her a happy future.

Lyndon stood up, and waved a quick farewell.

"'Bye, Violet. I'll be back soon." He smiled. "I'll find a way to keep you, alright? Even if I have to fight a war for you, I promise!"

* * *

To Lyndon, it seemed forever before the legal "war" was won, though it was only a matter of a month or so. The day came eventually when Grace—now called Violet Arnnu—was discharged from the hospital and Lyndon came to pick her up. He drove her home—to their apartment rooms in the city suburbs—and was delighted by her reactions to the front room, which had been cleaned especially for her, and her own bedroom. Violet's purple eyes sparkled in childish excitement as he showed her around though the little girl didn't say anything—but Lyndon's efforts were more than repaid, he felt, when suddenly she turned around and hugged him. Even more so later that evening, when she called him "Dad." Lyndon told himself that he had done the right thing.

They lived happily together in that apartment for a year or so, until Lyndon finished his college years and decided to move to another, bigger house that was farther out in the country, despite that it meant he would have to commute farther from home to work every day—he had earned his chemistry degree and now took a job at a laboratory located in the city. They were much happier there. Violet grew healthy and thriving, far excelling her classmates in physical strength and dexterity by the time she was ten. Her grades were outstanding as well. Meanwhile, though Lyndon's work became more and more stressful and attention-demanding as the time went by and he was promoted, he always managed to put on a bright face for Violet when they were at home. And finally there came a day when he explained to her, as he drove her home from school, that he had quit his job.

Violet, now a lively, bright-eyed girl of thirteen, thought he was joking at first. "Huh?" she questioned. "What do you mean, Dad?"

"'I've done all I wanted to do at that laboratory," Lyndon explained slowly.

"And I want to be free to carry on my life's real work. Violet? Do you remember anything? Anything at all?"

Violet bit her lip, thinking to herself how quiet and thoughtful her father had been lately. Perhaps this had something to do with it. But search her memory as she would, she couldn't remember anything from before she was seven, when she had suffered from amnesia. For, of course, that was what Lyndon meant.

"No," she admitted, shaking her head. "Why?"

* * *

"I never wanted to tell you, but you were always going to find out someday… and I think you've been getting old enough to wonder if I am really your father," Lyndon told her slowly, later that day, when she had finished her homework. They were sitting in the living room, and Violet had just been going out to ride her horse, Daisy, when Lyndon had stopped her.

Her fingers fumbled for an instant with the latch of her purple riding helmet, and she stared at the floor, almost afraid to look up. How did Lyndon know her recent misgivings?

"So you aren't?" she asked, finally looking up some seconds later.

Lyndon shook his head after a moment, his eyes strangely sad. "Your real parents were murdered years back, Violet. I… I felt that it was my duty to look after you." He sighed. "And that's partly why I quit my job today."

For the second time, Violet was startled. "What can that possibly have to do with my real parents?" she demanded, though her thoughts were elsewhere. Her parents…murdered?

"You see, Violet, I've decided to continue their work. They were scientists, and they were working on a special, top-secret project… What it was, I found out only five years ago," Lyndon admitted.

He stood up suddenly. "Come into my office, I have something to show you."

"But you never want me going in your office," Violet murmured aloud, following him automatically. She had forgotten all about going horse riding.

"Well, I think you're old enough now." Holding the door open for her, Lyndon smiled, and bowed slightly. "Walk right in."

Violet stepped into the room, and then stopped, looking around in amazement. She knew Lyndon was a scientist, but she hadn't been aware of the small-scale laboratory right in their own home.

Her purple eyes widened as she looked around with all the curious interest of a young teenager. There was everything she'd ever fancied to be in a real, full-scale laboratory, like the one Lyndon had worked at.

Tubes, devices, vials, bottles—everything. A shelf full of packages and containers labeled with chemical combinations. Violet was fascinated by the overwhelming purple in the room. There was almost every color imaginable in there, but almost an overabundance of purple. Violet's mind reeled.

Lyndon glanced down at her, smiling faintly though his eyes were serious. "This, Violet, is my life's work."

"What is?" she breathed.

He didn't answer at first. "I'm going to have some friends coming over as well, to help me work on this—Dr. Staunton, Dr. Pizzey, and Dr. Lafferty. You'll still be going to school and everything, but as you see, I will be working at home from now on. And you can hang out in the laboratory whenever you want, unless we're doing something dangerous."

"But what are you working on?" Violet whispered, wide-eyed.

"Vi, you've watched movies about what they call 'superhumans,' haven't you?" Lyndon asked her slowly. "You remember that one about the guy with a shield? How they gave him an injection and he became superstrong?"

"Um, yeah, I guess," Violet nodded, and suddenly her eyes lit up with realization. "Wait, but Dad—I mean—that's impossible!"

"It doesn't have to be." Lyndon bent down slightly, to be closer to her height. "And it won't be. Your parents had just finished their first attempt when they were murdered. They called it Trial 1—T1. But it didn't do much towards superhumanness, and besides, it wasn't permanent.

"But working for the same people, my friends and I were able to get our hands on a sample of that T1, and in the past four years, we have been developing a second attempt—T2. We succeeded a couple of weeks ago."

Suddenly Lyndon sighed. "And you know what? We succeeded so well that the boss got frightened. We're supposed to be coming up with a way to help stabilize patients' conditions for surgery and dangerous situations like that, but our T2 tests on animals have been strengthening them to the point that the boss says we've gone overboard."

He bit his lip. "He's calling the project off, wants us to go back to T1 and restart our research. But no, why would we do that?" Lyndon patted his coat pocket. "I have our research here, in computer chip form, as well as a sample, Violet.

"We aren't going to give up, Vi." Lyndon put a hand on her shoulder, his face serious. "We're going to continue our research—here. Can you imagine a world where everyone was superhuman, Vi?" His light blue eyes shone. "A world where there was no pain? Where everyone was healthy and perfect?"

Violet's eyes sparkled as well. "That sounds amazing," she breathed, and Lyndon nodded.

"Doesn't it?" A giant grin spread itself over Lyndon's face. "And that's the world we're going to create, Violet. It's going to take a long time, but I promise you, it'll happen within your lifetime!"

"You mean it?" Suddenly Violet found herself contemplating all sorts of possibilities for what she could do if she, herself, was one day superhuman. Her eyes lit up in excitement.

* * *

And so Dr. Barry Staunton, Dr. Brooks Pizzey, and Dr. Viator Lafferty joined the regular circle at the Arnnu home, Dr. Staunton often bringing his fifteen-year-old boy Louis, and also his daughter Rebecca, who was Violet's age. Together the scientists would test, experiment, argue, and test again, while the teenagers would either watch them or play together outside, sometimes even venturing to attempt to complete their homework together.

The years passed, three of them, until Louis Staunton graduated and Rebecca and Violet became seniors—though now Violet had playfully decided to change her name to "Trinity Ryder," and insisted everyone call her that, even at school. She gradually grew so serious about it that when she and her father began to discuss various college options, she opted to get in with that name. When she started college, she was a confident, almost proud girl whom her friends considered something of a genius. "Trinity Ryder" made purple her trademark, even dying her own brown hair that color. She was popular and everyone liked her.

As for Lyndon, his years of intense, careful work had changed him as well. He became increasingly devoted to what he considered his "duty" of producing a superhuman world, pouring all his energies, all his hopes, his dreams, and talents into the work—and into Violet's future. He became almost fanatic about her, eventually—when he and his confederates gradually came to realize they might have to wage a war to secure their objectives—holding her up as the only possible and capable leader of the victorious army, which would be their superhuman one.

He was the leader of the small scientist group as well, both intellectually and by popular vote. It was he who, in 2020, came up with the idea of taking the project underground, starting the process of collecting their army, and eventually staging bank robberies to fund their expensive projects. T3 had been closer to the mark, though it wasn't perfect; he was confident that T4 would be the final and complete culmination of their research.

Tabs were kept on the remaining members of the Foley family as well. There wasn't much to learn about them. They were sent to foster homes, and nothing ever came up about Grace.

Violet continued her schooling, getting into college a couple of years early, in the autumn of 2023. She came back for her second year in 2024, but this time the term was interrupted one day, and events would follow so quickly that she would never be at college again.

* * *

The lecture hall was giant, but only one of the many at this college. It was after school hours, so the seats were only half filled. Near the front of the room, the professor went through a demonstration of nuclear physics on the board. Most of the students in the room weren't fully paying attention, as attendance at this lecture was only for those who wanted to do better in class.

"Come on, we went over this last week." The teacher tapped the board with her pointer, making a few of the students jump and look up guiltily. "You have got to know this. Trinity Ryder?"

A tall, slim eighteen-year-old young woman stood up from her desk. Her shoulder-length hair, a dark brown, was dyed light purple at the tips, including her long bangs that hung over her face. She wore boots and a short skirt. Her light purple jacket, that matched her eyes, had the collars up.

"Fission is splitting up. Fusion is combining." Her voice was level, casual, and had a slight western accent.

"Very good," the teacher approved, as Trinity slipped back into her seat. "Everyone, you have simply got to memorize that. Now..."

Trinity's phone vibrated in her pocket, and she pulled it out, holding it underneath her desk.

Everything's ready for you to come home, Vi. When can we expect you?

Trinity sighed softly, and typed a quick answer.

Next weekend. See you soon, Dad.

She turned her phone off, and looked back up at the teacher and the board, but with new meaning in her strangely purple eyes. Idly she tapped her desk, as if impatient for the lecture to end...

Book Two: More than Friends

Annapolis, Maryland.
21 December 2024 A.D.
Whyte Home.

Lost in reverie about the Purple Blitzkrieg, Violet didn't notice as the remaining minutes flew by, till she heard voices in the living room. She perked up, and checked her watch; it was a few minutes short of six-thirty. She could hear the voices. There were Moira's excited, happy tones, and Conner's deeper ones. Then Darek's, the deepest of all. Giulia's Italian-accented, chirpy voice, and Erin's and Niamh's slight Irish accents. Joyce's strong, Texas-style American. The Montoyas' characteristic light tones, and the Marwicks' ironic ones. Percy and Mark Smyth's sarcastic voices mixing with their younger sister Lila's cheerfully spoken words. And a new voice, one she hadn't heard before, uttering happy and startled exclamations of delight.

Violet slipped down from the stool, noticing that the timer on the oven read only a few more seconds. Flipping herself over to it superhumanly, she turned off the timer just before it would go off. She pulled on oven mitts from the drawer next to it, and retrieved the macaroni and cheese from the oven, leaving it on the stove to cool.

The dinner was ready. Violet tiptoed over to the doorway to the living room, pausing with her hand on the doorknob.

All the voices mingled together, and suddenly Violet felt overwhelmed.

They were all so friendly and happy. Surely she didn't belong here. Or did she?

But someone had already seen her and pulled the door open, introducing her to the assembly. They turned to look at her, but Violet glanced first at the one who'd opened the door, the one she knew best out of all of them.

Their eyes met, and Violet smiled...

"Hey, Vi," Conner smiled back. Then he glanced away from her and at his mother. "Mom, this is Violet. Vi..."

"Hello, Mrs. Whyte," Violet smiled politely.

Mrs. Whyte was standing between Conner and Moira, and upon seeing the new arrival, she held out her hands welcomingly. "It's nice to meet you, Violet," she told the tall, slim, brown-haired eighteen-year-old. Conner had told his mother vaguely about their meeting the young woman during the "Purple Blitzkrieg," as people were now calling the events with Encephalon; Moira had told their mother nothing at all about this girl who was obviously friends with both the twins. But she seemed alright to Mrs. Whyte.

Violet's polite smile turned real, and to everyone's surprise, she impulsively hugged Mrs. Whyte. Then, as if embarrassed of herself, she turned and darted back into the kitchen. "Moira—the dinner's ready."

* * *

For a while, there was talk about Violet's going back to college, but she hung around Annapolis until the Whyte family was made as complete as it had been in years, when Mr. Whyte's finally returned home from Washington. And then, still, she did not go, as Moira found out while talking to her brother one spring evening.

"She got a job here last week," he told her. He was playing tennis with himself against the side of the house. *Thump, thump.* "At the store down the street."

Moira's eyes narrowed slightly as she watched her brother. It was so strange seeing him taller than her, and she was mainly just glad he wasn't usually one to tease. "How'd you find that out?"

Conner shrugged. "I saw her there the other day. Why?" he asked, tossing the ball again, and harder.

"I dunno," Moira admitted. "But I thought she was going back to Texas or wherever she comes from."

"She says she never really liked it at college," Conner went on. "She wants to try to get a normal life."

"She'd be more normal if she just finished college," Moira muttered before she told herself sharply that it was none of her business.

"Did *you* ever want to be normal?" Conner asked his older sister quietly. "Just like everyone else?"

"No," Moira had to concede. "But *you* did, Conner, and you can't deny it. Yet you don't care how different you are now, do you," she observed. "And you're not going to make me think that Violet really wants to be, either. What changed about you?" She winced. "Is it because you're *above* normal now?"

Conner's face tightened slightly. "You don't understand," he told Moira. "None of us can ever be 'normal' anymore. But there's no reason to let that hold us back. Vi's free to live her own life. She's got newer and better goals now, more realistic ones. And that's what she's doing."

"How do you know that?" Moira raised her eyebrows.

Conner half-smiled. "We talk on the phone. You've got her number, too, right?"

"No," Moira shook her head emphatically.

Suddenly Conner caught the tennis ball a final time and dropped it into his pocket, heading for the door to their house. "Maybe you should get it, then. Really, Moira, Vi's trying to be a new person."

"Conner, do you realize what she's done to us—to *you?*" Moira demanded before she could stop herself. "What she does now, doesn't matter. We shouldn't talk to her."

"Give her a chance, Moira," Conner returned with a quiet disappointment Moira had never heard before, and she glanced at him in surprise. But he was looking away from her. "How's she supposed to find her way back into society if no one is there to open the door for her?"

His eyes met hers briefly. "And if you can accept me, Moira, then you can accept her."

With that, he disappeared into the house. For a moment, Moira looked like she would follow him, while some heated emotion twisted her face; but then she shoved her hands into her blue coat pockets—formerly her younger brother's—and marched off resolutely, staring at her breath in the cold air as she walked down the street.

Sometimes it was like she didn't even know Conner anymore, and Moira hated that. Now, as she thought about it, she bit her lip. Was it just Moira's prejudices, or was she right that Violet Arnnu still felt a connection to Conner?

Because Moira didn't like that at *all*. Conner wasn't a drugged robot soldier anymore—he was her brother again, and he wasn't supposed to be standing up for someone like Violet Arnnu. Moira might have forgiven her—but she didn't trust her.

But Conner is his own person, she reminded herself in an effort to calm down. *He makes his own decisions. It's none of my business whom he talks to.*

Moira still felt like going to see Violet and telling her rather violently to leave her brother alone. But that would only complicate matters. So, instead, Moira went on a walk. Walking made everything better sometimes.

* * *

Yet Moira would probably have been even more annoyed had she known that at their graduations a year and a half later, Violet would be one of the loudest to cheer them both. But by that time, many of Moira's suspicions had disappeared, and she greeted the tall twenty-year-old brunette with almost as much enthusiasm as did Conner.

The twins were eighteen now, and—unfortunately, in Moira's mind—Conner had grown even taller. He was even taller than Violet. So the two Whytes presented a rather humorous picture for the many cameras that wanted to capture them and their classmates on this their special day.

But finally they escaped—only to run into Violet, who laughed, snapped another photo, and told the twins that their parents were waiting for them.

"Stop shooting," Conner laughed at her before turning to follow Moira.

"Haha," Violet laughed back.

Apparently she didn't have anything to do after attending the ceremony, because she was still around even after congratulating the twins. But just then Moira felt someone tap her shoulder, and she wheeled around to see her best friend Lucinda.

"We're done!" Lucinda giggled helplessly. Her cap was awry and her hair was rather mussed up, but her face was perfectly happy. "We've *finished!*"

Beaming, Moira threw her arms around her friend. "Yeah!"

"Are you doing anything tonight?" Lucinda asked her friend.

Moira shrugged. "Just dinner, I think. Mom's got the party planned for next Saturday. Why?"

Her friend grinned. "Some friends and I were going to hang out and go shopping," she explained. "I was wondering if you'd be interested."

"Probably," Moira had to agree. "Who's coming?"

"All our old group," Lucinda winked. "It's not a lot. I mean... Cloe and I were planning to go out together, and she's convinced Nina to come, too... And we're going to have dinner at Pervitto's."

"I'm in," Moira declared enthusiastically.

Lucinda nodded. "What about Conner?"

"I..." Moira glanced around, her eyes narrowing as she saw her brother standing some yards away, talking to...Violet. Moira's face hardened.

"Is something wrong?" Lucinda followed Moira's gaze, seeing Conner first and then whom the new graduate was talking to. "Wait, is that—"

"Nothing's wrong," Moira sighed, but her voice seemed a bit unusually tight. "Come on, let's go. Conner's not coming."

"But you didn't ask him," Lucinda protested. "And is that—"

"Yes, it's *her*," Moira had to admit. "And as we can see, my brother is too busy talking to her to hang out with any of his school friends, or even with us. It's not worth asking him if he wants to come."

"I mean, we could ask Violet, too," Lucinda suggested quietly.

But Moira shook her head decisively. "It's not worth it. Let's just go. I'd better tell my parents first, though," she added quickly. "I'll catch up with you and the other two. When are we leaving?"

Finally Lucinda tore her gaze away from Conner and Violet. She smiled at

Moira. "As soon as you're back."

***

"Yes. That's him."

Conner held up his hand to try to shield his eyes from the early afternoon sun as he glanced in the direction his older friend had been pointing. "He doesn't look too much out of the ordinary."

Violet shrugged. "Maybe he doesn't, but I know I've seen him hanging around your house at least three times now. And unless he lives in your area…"

"No, he doesn't." Conner scrutinized the short, dark-haired man who was decked out in a baseball cap and sunglasses. He couldn't help but notice that the stalker-suspect wasn't talking to anyone at the graduation reception. It was only too clear that no one there knew him.

"I'd know him if he did. And I haven't seen him before, at least not for more than a passing glance. But I feel that if I'd run into him during the Blitzkrieg, I would've known."

"My thoughts exactly," Violet nodded approvingly. "So he's new to the area, very clearly suspicious…and definitely watching your family, Trooper."

Conner bit his lip. "Do you have to call me that?"

"Sorry." But Violet didn't sound very apologetic, and Conner wasn't paying much attention to her tone of voice anyway.

"What could he possibly be watching us for?" Conner muttered to himself. "We could go tackle him to try to find out, but then again he could be with the government…and that could be bad."

"Very bad," the twenty-year-old young woman had to agree. "So do we just ignore him, then?"

"I don't know," Conner sighed. "If only we knew whether or not he's actually with the government."

"Whatever he is, he's certainly very professional," Violet murmured. "Well, I'll leave it up to you, then. Not like you need my help, anyway."

"Are you annoyed at me or something?" Conner turned to glance at her, his face confused.

"Why would I be?" Violet shrugged. She smiled. "I'm just tired."

"Maybe you shouldn't work so hard," Conner pondered. "Your job sounds pretty stressful... Maybe you should've gone back to college after all."

"Nah, I'd just stay up even later if I was studying," Violet laughed. "And they wouldn't want me at any college, anyway."

She frowned. "Everyone knows I don't really belong. Maybe...maybe it would've been better if Dad hadn't—"

"He was trying to save you," Conner shook his head. "He was the one who got you into the scheme, after all. You told me that."

"No, I'm just as guilty as the next, and more guilty than most." Violet shook her head. "No one is going to let me forget that, and I'm not sure that I'd *want* to forget it, either."

She sighed. "But I wish people would give me another chance."

Her younger friend shrugged. "I've given you another chance, even if no one else has. Of course, my opinion isn't worth anything, but..."

"No." Again, Violet shook her head. "Your opinion is worth everything."

Conner's eyes narrowed as he stared in confusion, but Violet kept on going.

"Somehow it has always seemed that way to me," she murmured. "From the very start, I didn't want you to stay locked up in that robot, you know. I wanted to know your name. I wanted to know what you thought. I wanted to know...*you.*"

Conner half-laughed. "But—"

"But nothing." She took his hand lightly, turning it so they could both see his palm. "You thought I couldn't care less? Well, I could've. Those hands that saved my life multiple times. The man—no, the boy—that I called *Trooper.* I always wanted to know what was inside."

She dropped his hand, smiling sadly. "I never told you that before. I didn't think you would believe me. Not after all that."

"Why wouldn't I believe you?" Conner asked, after a moment's quiet. "You know what I told my sister. You may be a murderer, and a criminal, but you, Vi, aren't a liar. That's just something you never were." He smiled back. "Is that why you still call me Trooper sometimes?"

"No," she answered abruptly, turning away. "That's just habit. A habit I need to break."

"It's okay," Conner murmured. "I didn't realize what the word meant for you. To me, it just means a nightmare not worth remembering except to regret."

She half-turned towards him. "Well, for me, it's the name of my human guardian angel. An angel that I knew existed, that I even saw...but that I didn't know, until now. That's what the word means to me."

"Call me Trooper, then," Conner told her. "I won't mind."

Her eyebrows shot up as the confusion in her purple eyes doubled. "You can't be serious."

"But I am," Conner laughed.

Violet shook her head in disbelief before glancing away again. "Well, then, Trooper. Do you happen to have any idea where and with whom your sister is going? Because Mr. Stalker is following them."

"She's going somewhere?" Conner peered out over the crowd again, a task that was easy for him because of his outstanding (literally) height. "Oh, she's with her friends. But...where are they going?"

"That might be something to find out," Violet shrugged. "Because...yeah."

Conner had his phone out before he'd stopped nodding. It was a few more seconds before he was on the phone with Moira, but it was still soon enough. In the meantime, Violet kept her eyes on the group and pursuer.

"Hey, Moira," Conner spoke quickly into the phone once his sister had answered. "Yeah, it's me, of course. Mind if I ask what's up?"

* * *

"Good. He still knows I exist," Moira muttered to herself. "Nothing," she answered the question, as her friends glanced at her curiously. "The girls and I are going shopping and then out to dinner at Giulia's place. Want to come?"

"Umm, no thanks, sorry, and no offense to Giulia," Conner answered after a pause. What Moira didn't know was that Violet had gestured to Conner to answer in the negative.

Moira's scowl deepened. "Alright, then. I'll see you sometime, I guess."

"Okay. And also, Moira, uh—" Conner's sentence was abruptly broken off.

"Eh?" Moira asked absently.

"Um, nothing," Conner said after a moment. "Okay. See you soon. Bye."

"That wasn't nothing," Moira began sharply, but she broke off in disgust as her brother hung up.

"The nerve!" she bit out, shoving her phone back into her pocket.

"What's wrong?" Cloe wondered.

"He's not hanging out with her again, is he?" Nina raised her eyebrows. "I thought she'd be gone by now."

"Well, she isn't," Moira shook her head angrily. "If only she was!"

"You sound just as annoyed as you used to be," Lucinda remarked thoughtfully. "Is something going on?"

Moira bit her lip.

"Yes, but I don't know *what.* That's exactly the problem. I just don't know."

* * *

"Why didn't you want me to tell her?" Conner asked, surprised, as he put his phone away. "And *why* shouldn't we have gone with them?"

"We can follow them more secretively if we're not really part of the group." Violet was already moving. "And I don't want them to panic."

"I see." Conner nodded once or twice. "We're going to let that man follow them. And you and I are going to follow *him.*"

"Exactly, Trooper, exactly." Violet smiled approvingly. "We've got this."

* * *

"I can't believe you're actually trying that on," Lucinda laughed. "Are you planning on buying it?"

"Not really," Moira admitted, laughing herself. "But you girls can get a few shots of me wearing it. Hope that makes you happy."

"Definitely," Nina giggled. "Okay, there's an empty changing room. Go on

28

and do your thing, Moira!"

"See you," Moira grinned as she stepped into the small room and shut and locked the door behind her. She hung the store dress on the hook in back of the door, but instead of beginning to take off her outer clothes, Moira instead reached for her phone and began typing away busily.

She appeared strangely nervous and excited. Her hands shook as she typed. "Come on, come on, Moira, concentrate," she muttered to herself as she typed one word wrong, over and over again. Finally she'd successfully corrected it, and after one brief read-through, Moira hit the button to send the message.

Dear Mrs. Marwick, can you please call Nina and Cloe right away and tell them to come home? They're fine right now but I'm not sure things will stay that way, and I don't want to frighten them. Right away please. Thanks so much.

She sent nearly the same message to Lucinda's mother, and then took off her jacket, tying it around her waist. Next she took out a pair of sunglasses and fitted them over her face, nodding at the image she presented in the mirror.

"Finally," she murmured to herself as she heard her friends' ringtones from outside.

"Hello? Hello, Mom?" Nina asked quietly, and Lucinda did almost the exact same thing immediately afterwards. Moira bit her lip as she imagined how they must be signaling suspiciously to each other, but this was the best she could manage.

"Home...now...okay, I guess. What's wrong? Oh, okay. I'll see you then. Yes, we're leaving right now." Nina hung up. "Moira, Cloe and I have to go home now."

"Are you serious?" Moira demanded with convincing disbelief. "Right now?"

"Right now," Nina sighed. "Sorry, girl."

"That's me, too," Lucinda put in. "Are you sure your mom isn't calling you, too, Moira? This looks suspicious to me."

"Maybe she is," Moira admitted. "I'll check in a minute."

"Well, buy the dress if you like it, I guess," Cloe muttered.

"See you soon, Moira. I guess sooner than we think."

"Hopefully." Moira kept her tones light. "See you, girls."

"Bye."

"Goodbye!"

As soon as she was sure they were gone, Moira let out a sigh of semi-relief, semi-fright. "Okay, *that's* done. I hope he's after me, not them." She bit her lip. "Now to contact the police."

Contact the police she did, and her family as well. Moira was certain to phrase her situation lightly so as not to terrify her parents, while at the same time she didn't spare to give her brother the stark truth: she was being followed.

Even then, his answer didn't surprise her much, as Moira's brain had always been quick to jump to conclusions.

We know, he said.

You and Vi? Moira typed back. *But don't worry about it, because I've called the cops.*

Good, her brother returned. *So we don't need to hang around, then?*

Moira's face contorted as the realization of another possibility hit her, one she hadn't thought of yet. Conner and Violet had been...following the stalker?

How weak do they think I am!

I'm fine, she told her brother. *You two follow the Marwicks and Lucinda home and make sure they get there safe.*

Having said that, Moira slipped her phone back into her skirt pocket. She could hear the sounds of police sirens from outside the front of the store. Finally daring to step outside the changing room, Moira left the dress behind and hurried towards the store entrance, muttering to herself that "That was fast."

"Moira Whyte?" she could hear an officer asking startled store workers. "Is there a Moira Whyte in trouble here?"

"That's me," Moira answered loudly and quickly, stepping out from behind a clothes rack. "I'm here. I'm good."

"There you are," the officer nodded, smiling. "You're sure you're alright?"

Moira laughed nervously, wiping her brow in relief. "Yeah. I'm fine. They... haven't tried anything yet. Maybe they weren't going to. I don't know."

"But as you put it, the man has followed you to at least three stores at this point," the officer went on cheerily. Moira frowned—he didn't need to be so public about it. "Well. Want a free ride?"

The girl started. "I—"

"To your house, of course," the policeman laughed. "I'm kidding you."

Moira could hear murmuring from the crowd of interrupted shoppers around her, but she stepped forward anyway. "Y—yeah, I guess," she replied, especially since her knees still felt a little wobbly. "I mean, yes please. Thank you."

"No problem." The young officer flashed a grin. "Step right this way, Miss Whyte."

* * *

"So she called the police," Conner sighed as he watched his sister step into a police car down the street, "and they're giving her a ride home. I guess that was the sensible thing to do."

"Does that mean the stalker wasn't working with the government?" Violet reasoned. "Maybe we should've taken him down, then."

"There's no guarantee, and besides, calling the police is what any ordinary civilian would do," Conner pointed out. "At any rate, he's gone now."

"That's suspicious." Violet scowled. "Come to think of it, he was gone even before the police arrived."

The two glanced at each other.

"Coincidence?" Conner murmured after a moment, watching the police car and waving to his sister as she was driven away. She waved back, and Conner smiled, his worries temporarily lifted.

"Probably," Violet shrugged after a moment. "Your sister wanted us to follow her friends home, didn't she?" She cracked her knuckles slowly, one by one. "Never would've thought I'd be doing *this* for a living. But such is life."

"It isn't for a living, isn't it?" But Conner was distracted by something else. "Why do you always have to peek over my shoulder whenever I take a call or answer a text?"

The young woman giggled. "Obvious eavesdropping is better than concealed eavesdropping, isn't it? And besides, it wasn't important and you would've told me anyway. If it was secret, I wouldn't have done that."

Conner sighed. "Alright, then. Well, are we going, then?"

"One moment. Why is another police car coming?" Violet frowned as the vehicle drew closer to the storefront. "And with lights blazing, too."

Conner's brow furrowed. "I haven't the foggiest idea," he admitted. "Let's go see."

But as the two drew closer, they found the new police arrivals, too, searching for "Moira Whyte."

"The police came already," Conner spoke up once he got the chance. "I saw them leave. I'm the caller's brother. Conner Whyte."

"The police came already?" the officer echoed, question marks written all over his face as he shook his head. "No, kid. No, they didn't."

* * *

"Your name sounds familiar," the officer who was driving remarked to himself, after half a minute of fast and skillful driving.

"Does it?" Moira tilted her head slightly.

"Yes...let me just try to remember. Moira Whyte... Oh, you have something to do with the Blitzkrieg, don't you."

"Perhaps." Moira's eyes narrowed into slits. "Why?"

But the officer ignored her question, and Moira tried to resign herself to the fact that she'd caught a ride with a pleasant, social type of police officer. *Like Darek, a bit, I guess.* That thought was comforting, and suddenly Moira didn't find it so hard to smile anymore.

"You were one of the American fighters, weren't you?" The officer grinned at her in the rear-view mirror. "That's awesome, girl. That's awesome. And how old are you again, Miss Whyte?"

"Eighteen," Moira returned. "And I was sixteen then."

The officer shook his head in disbelief. "Amazing. You must be sharp."

"Must I?" The girl raised her eyebrows slightly.

And suddenly she saw, in the corner of the rear-view mirror, the officer's grin change to something of a smirk. "But not sharp enough, Miss Whyte. Not sharp enough."

Moira nodded slowly, but this time her gaze was down on her phone as she swiftly and silently pulled it out. But a sudden word from the previously silent second officer interrupted her, and she glanced up to find herself staring directly at a handgun with a silencer on the end.

"Give me the phone. And if you hit send, you're dead," the man growled. Moira noticed the scar across his cheek for the first time.

But she smiled tightly. "I don't need to. Here," she went on, passing the cell phone to him.

The man noticed with satisfaction that she had barely begun to type, but with alarm that she'd already received a message—from her brother.

U r in trouble. Stay calm.

"Good, we're all on the same page now. Drive faster, Myers. Alright, now I'm going to call your brother, and you're going to keep your mouth shut unless I say otherwise," the man continued. "Get it?"

Moira nodded stiffly, her face suddenly grim.

The man put the call through, then switched the phone to speakerphone.

"Moira? Moira, are you okay?" came Conner's voice after about two seconds. "Just let me talk to her, Vi!—I know what to say."

"This is an abductor, Mr. Whyte," the officer said after a moment. "Are you listening?"

"Let my sister go, or I'll—you haven't *hurt* her, have you?"

"Not yet." There was a soft, ruthless chuckle. "And I won't, as long as you follow my instructions." The man frowned as muffled sounds came across the call. "Who else is listening—your girlfriend?"

"No!" Conner spluttered. "I mean, no, she's not—not my 'girlfriend,' but she *is* listening—no, you're not! Yes, I'm sure!—*Ow!*"

"I have a serious message for you, Mr. Whyte, and I'm not going to wait forever to deliver it."

Moira bit her lip.

"Yeah, I'm listening, man. You let my sister go. Otherwise I'll hunt you down until I find you, and then—"

"Keep your mouth shut unless I ask for an answer, Trooper A1," the man hissed into the phone, and Moira started. "You don't have time to hunt me down, unfortunately. Here, Miss Whyte, now say something."

"Hey, Conner." Moira struggled to keep her voice perfectly calm, being well aware that any tension in her voice might betray weakness to her captors.

"Moira!" Conner shouted through the phone. "Where are you?"

"I'm fine," Moira answered, knowing that she'd likely have been punished for actually telling Conner where she was—that the game might have even ended, there and then. "Don't worry about me. And don't try running to keep up—I think we're going close to speeding." She smiled, a small, tight, strained smile. "I'm safe. They haven't hurt me."

"Don't get hurt, whatever you do," Conner told his sister anxiously. "We'll get you out of there."

"Okay." Moira swallowed hard. "Goodbye, I guess."

"See you soon," her brother put in hopefully.

"Good enough?" the officer broke in, his voice impatient. "She's alive. For now."

"Name your terms," Conner returned.

Suddenly the officer smiled. "Your sister isn't our target, Mr. Whyte. It's you. To be more precise, it's your blood. Do you understand that?"

There was a pause, but then Conner answered. "I'll do anything to get my sister back safe." From how he spoke, Moira could almost visualize his face—jaw set resolutely.

"This is what we'll do, then." The kidnapper took a deep breath. "You're going to let yourself get kidnapped as well and temporarily put to sleep. We will collect a sample or two, and then leave you and your sister where the police will find you. It's that simple."

Another short pause. "What do you need my blood for?"

"You'll find that out later. What matters now is that your sister's life is in danger. You have until dawn tomorrow to comply—and two hours to give me your final answer. I'll call you back then, understand?"

"Understood."

Abruptly hanging up, the officer nodded once to himself before tossing Moira's phone out the window.

"Hey!" Moira exclaimed angrily.

Pulling a small box out of his pocket, the officer shrugged. "Like I don't realize you'd have a tracker on that thing?"

"But…" Moira bit her lip. "Anyway, you're not going to succeed with whatever your plan is. It's only too obvious that you want my brother's blood simply for the T4. Yet you can't attack him directly, because he's too strong, so you're using me. But I'm not going to let him make that choice." Slowly and carefully, Moira reached down, towards her right sneaker.

"Except he doesn't have a choice, and neither do you."

The man's voice sounded strangely close to her own ear. Moira looked up, only to have her head forced down again by a strong left hand.

She felt the sting in her neck even without seeing the needle. But the pain lasted only a few seconds before the dosage took effect and Moira slumped over in the back seat, unconscious. The officer smiled slightly as he replaced the needle-case in his pocket.

"Good driving," he complimented the now-silent driver. "We're almost there."

* * *

Conner stared at his phone as the dial tone sounded, and slowly, finally, he put it away.

"There's only one reason they'd want my blood," he muttered. "T4."

Yet, looking around, Conner was surprised to find that Violet was already in action, talking to one of the real police officers. Quickly, Conner walked over.

"Yes, that number does belong to one of our cars," the officer was nodding as he glanced at the device in his hand. "Driven by Officer Meyer."

"Who else?" Violet raised one eyebrow.

"No one else," the officer shook his head. "He currently drives solo."

"But…there were two men in that car," Conner broke in. "I saw them."

"Right. Can't you track the car?" Violet went on.

"We can." For the first time, the officer smiled. "We're already on it. I'll let you know as soon as we get results." He glanced at Conner. "Mr. Whyte, and...?"

"No one," Violet shrugged, turning quickly to go. "Come on, Conner! We've got to discuss this."

"We can't give them T4 blood," Conner told her quietly, yet urgently, as the two walked away together. "We just can't. That'd start some real trouble."

"And your sister's being in danger isn't real trouble?" Violet returned impassively. "That man on the phone is Callum Ranvier, and he's a professional. In case you don't remember him."

"Remember him?" Conner stared. "Why would I? *How* would I?"

"I guess you only met him once, and it was while you were under the drug," Violet realized. She sighed. "He was one of my father's strongest supporters. He's got a strong left hand, too. But if I recall correctly, he never took the superhuman dose. He worked mainly in espionage and propaganda—he definitely wasn't a scientist or a doctor."

"Is that why he wants T4 now?" Conner mused. "Well, that just makes the situation worse."

"Especially if he's got other professionals with him." Violet frowned.

Conner glanced at his friend, the first wave of suspicion crossing his face. "How did they find out which vehicle it was?"

"The license number," Violet returned shortly.

Conner raised his eyebrows. "You memorized it? Why?"

"It was suspicious from the beginning," Violet admitted. "The police arrived much too soon. As if they were waiting for the call. And even before that, the initial stalker had disappeared."

"So you're telling me you already had an idea of what was going on, and you didn't tell me." Conner shook his head in disbelief. "We could've saved Moira."

"We didn't have any evidence, and there was no time," Violet tried to excuse herself. "Besides, you wouldn't have wanted to confront or even attack officials—"

"You knew the first stalker was a professional from the beginning, didn't you." Conner bit his lip as he stopped walking. "But you didn't tell me that, either."

"If I'd mentioned the possibility, you would've concluded that he was working with the government," Violet returned a bit heatedly. "But you concluded that anyway, and that's why we couldn't have ended this two hours ago."

"The whole point of following Moira was to make sure nothing happened!" Conner nearly shouted. "And now it has, and we had a chance to stop it! You should've told me!"

"Well, I'm sorry!" Violet's voice rose in turn. "Hopefully next time your sister will recognize a trap before she walks into it! And this isn't even the first time!"

Conner began to say something, then broke off and tried again. For a moment he stared in angry, forced silence; then the words came out slowly.

"My sister isn't stupid."

"I didn't say she was." Violet, too, fought to keep her temper. "Anyway, all we can do now is try to fix this—"

"How are we supposed to work together if you don't even tell me what's going on?" Conner shook his head. "We wouldn't even *be* in this situation if you'd told me! What else do I need to know?"

"You need to know that you have two hours to figure out how you're going to deal with this," Violet returned flatly. "Since you don't want my help."

But Conner was still too fired up to reply calmly. "If you don't want to help, I'm fine with that," he gritted. "Perfectly fine."

"Right, and your sister wouldn't want me to help anyway." Violet's eyes flashed, and her words sounded bitter even to Conner. "So what are you going to do, Conner Whyte?"

Conner's deep blue eyes peered straight into Violet's purple ones, and he scowled.

"I'll find that out for myself, Violet Arnnu," he gritted. "Maybe we'll tell you about it when it's all over."

"Alright, I don't care." Violet shrugged, a movement that was strangely hard. "Bye."

Yet she stood still, almost as if she was waiting for Conner to change his mind.

But the angry eighteen-year-old didn't. "Bye," he shot back, turning and marching away with the quick, long stride he'd grown accustomed to as a Violet Army soldier.

Violet's mouth opened, as if she would call him back, but then something new came into her eyes, and she turned away, walking slowly in the other direction.

Is this what it's like? she wondered.

* * *

The first thing Moira heard was the voice.

"Good. I'm glad you've realized that this is your only option." The words had been spoken by her primary captor, Moira realized dimly, at the same time as she realized she was tied to a chair. Her eyes flew open, and she glanced about wildly, barely giving her eyes enough time to adjust to the sudden feeling of re-consciousness.

She was in a small, normal, very low-ceilinged household room that had been cleared of any furniture besides the chair, though the lack of windows made Moira suspect that she was being held in a basement. The second "officer" was the only other person in the room, leaning against the door frame and talking to someone on the phone—probably Conner, Moira surmised.

She let her eyes fall shut again, aware that the officer didn't know she was awake. There was nothing like having an element of surprise, no matter how small.

And yet she felt her pulse shoot up as she listened to the phone call. She was very definitely in trouble.

"So this is how it will work, Mr. Whyte. After I get off the phone, I'm going to inject your sister with a dosage of Myelin. You remember what that is, no? So you do."

Moira felt her blood run cold, even before the threatened dosage. *She* definitely remembered Myelin, from the Blitzkrieg. It was what had nearly killed Joyce Liszt.

"To put it plainly, Mr. Whyte, after this call, we will have about twenty minutes before it's too late to save your sister. In order to accomplish this, you need to let yourself be captured by my men. If you walk down the street, they'll find you. It's as simple as that. But you're not to attack them, and you're to let them put you out without any trouble. Don't think about trying to trick us, because you haven't got the time. That's all I have to say. You have up to five minutes to head outside.

"I'll see you soon, Mr. Whyte. Call me back if you have any questions."

With that, Callum Ranvier hung up. He paused a minute before walking over to Moira's chair. The eighteen-year-old swallowed hard as she kept hanging her head low, trying to maintain the illusion of her being asleep. But it didn't work.

"You're awake, aren't you?" Callum asked softly, close to her ear. Moira's eyes flew open, and she bit her lip as she stared at the syringe in her captor's latex-gloved hand.

"So you heard the call, too." Callum sounded relieved. "That's nice; I don't have to repeat myself."

"Why are you doing this?" Moira choked.

"It's nothing personal," Callum shrugged. "Don't think of it that way. I'm not really hurting any of you kids. But this is the only way I can get my hands on the superhuman dosage. Then I'll be out of your lives. You'll never see me again." He glanced at Moira and the chair, and sighed. "You'll probably last longer if you're lying down, won't you."

"Maybe." Moira sounded dubious.

"Alright." Suddenly Callum set the syringe down, pulling out the needle case from his belt. Quickly he selected one, and stepped closer to Moira, sticking it in her arm without giving her a chance to react. Moira flinched, but Callum smiled.

"This is just so I don't have to worry about you attacking me if I let you out of that chair," he explained. "Get it? I think it'll also make it hurt less, as well, so there you go. I don't want to hurt you."

"Fine," Moira gritted. She could tell that she had less control over her movements, but at least she wasn't passing out.

Over the course of the next two minutes, Moira found herself on the carpeted floor. Having taken the precaution of the first injection, her captor didn't bother to restrain her, but instead took up the syringe again, lightly touching the tip of the needle to Moira's wrist. The girl shut her eyes tightly.

"It's only until your brother gets here," Callum reminded her. Then he began injecting the fluid.

Moira's arm half-twisted, and her face contorted as her arm began shaking. Callum appeared startled, but finally he pulled the syringe away.

"That should be enough," he murmured. "And I don't think you need a bandage. Do you want one, anyway?"

But Moira didn't answer him, and his phone began to ring just about then, so Callum Ranvier quickly left the room, locking the door behind him.

Moira's eyes flashed back open, and slowly, groggily, she pulled herself to a sitting position, then stared at her left arm, which had suddenly and quite curiously stopped shaking. Moira bit her lip, watching until the first tinges of blue began to appear, just under her skin.

"Hang it!" she breathed, suddenly leaping into action. "It wasn't enough!"

* * *

In her apartment, Violet had been pacing for the last hour, sometimes sitting down, but always standing up again. And yet, when her phone finally began to ring, she paused two entire seconds before answering it.

"I'm sorry," was the first thing she said. "I'm sorry, okay?"

"I'm sorry, too," came Conner's voice. "But Vi...I'm...worried about my sister."

Violet bit her lip. "Ranvier called, didn't he?"

"He did." Conner sighed. "Vi, he's just injected Moira with Myelin. I—we haven't got much time left. I have to let myself get captured in the next three minutes. I just wanted to say..."

"Myelin?" Violet muttered. "The sneak. But Conner, I'll get captured instead."

"Are you crazy?" Conner demanded across the phone. "It's dangerous! And if Ranvier knows you—"

"He'd probably love to kill me, even if he doesn't seem to care for revenge on you or Moira," Violet mused. "But I don't care. It's dangerous for you, too. And I'm not letting you get hurt."

"She's my sister, Violet!"

"And I'm willing to do anything to keep you safe, Trooper!" Violet gritted. "Even if you're mad at me now." Suddenly her eyes opened wide as she remembered something.

"I'm not mad at you—"

"Besides, you're forgetting something, and so is Ranvier." Violet took a deep breath. "What blood type is your sister, again? Isn't she an A?"

"Why does that matter?" Conner spluttered.

"So you don't even remember why you had to take my blood to save Joyce Liszt. Myelin restoration is blood type-specific," Violet reminded him, her face dark.

"Oh no," Conner breathed as he, too, realized. "Oh no. How can we save Moira?"

"By taking my suggestion." Violet's voice was decisive. "It's the only way. Even you should be able to see that."

There was a short, quiet pause.

"I'll tell Ranvier," Conner gave in finally. "Even he will have to understand. But are you sure you can do this, because Ranvier probably hates you—"

"You didn't ask me that when you wanted to save Joyce," Violet broke in. "Why ask now? I'm just glad you're realizing that sometimes, to protect the people you love, you've got to take the law into your own hands. But I expect you to be on their heels, Conner Whyte!"

"I'll do it," Conner affirmed. "I'll do it. Anything else?"

Suddenly Violet laughed, a bit nervously. "Do you think Moira will like me after this?"

* * *

Yet Conner's and Violet's plans went wrong from the very beginning.

Callum's men surrounded Violet, as they'd been told to. They knocked her unconscious. And then Conner found out how Callum intended to save Moira's life—Violet was whisked away in a police car, lights blazing and siren screaming.

He couldn't even stay in sight for more than two minutes. Then he was done.

Conner shook his head in near-despair as he finally came to a stop, panting for breath as his blood raced and his head pounded.

How was he supposed to keep up? At least there was a slight chance that Conner could find them after all. It just depended on how hard they'd searched Violet.

The eighteen-year-old pulled out his phone, and after a few moments, broke into nervous, relieved laughter. On his screen was a map, and on that map a red dot was moving rapidly away from him. But it had already taken a few turns, so Conner knew the general direction the vehicle must be taking. He smiled to himself. The kidnappers would have to follow the street layout, but Conner wasn't restricted in any such way.

"I'm coming," he murmured briefly before clenching his hand more tightly around his phone and then taking off running like a madman.

* * *

"Good, finally." Callum sighed as he slid yet another syringe needle into unconscious Violet's wrist. "I think we're nearly out of time. Is this enough to save her?" he asked, holding up the nearly-filled syringe for one of his companions to inspect.

The man shrugged. "You'd know better than I would."

"I'm not a doctor," Callum muttered. "Alright, then. I guess we'll find out."

He straightened away from the limp form on the stretcher, heading towards the door to the room Moira had been contained in; then Callum paused. His eyes hardened as he glanced at Violet again.

"Whatever you do, don't let her wake up," he warned the other three. "We're not done. And I don't know if I want to let her go anyway. I wasn't expecting to actually run into the one who turned things upside down a year and a half ago." He smiled vaguely. "No, I'd like to have at least one conversation first."

"Alright," they agreed.

Callum turned back to the door, unlocking it and pausing half an instant before starting to pull it open.

He was surprised to find the room shrouded in darkness, but that didn't deter him long. He simply called to his companions for a light, though he didn't wait for them before he stepped carefully into the room.

After a few seconds, his eyes had somewhat adjusted, and he bent down over Moira's limp form. The man blinked a couple of times; something wasn't right. Moira's eyes were shut, and she was breathing heavily, but her left sleeve was torn, both her face and her left arm were bleeding, and even in the dim light Callum could see that her skin was still its original color.

"What the—" he began.

His words were cut short almost literally as Moira's right hand suddenly shot out, her fingers clenching a large shard of broken glass. She'd been aiming for Callum's hand, but the glass sank into his forearm instead.

"Help!" Callum managed to shout at the top of his lungs, before Moira finished her primary attack by snatching up another piece of glass from the floor, scrambling to her feet, and kicking Callum's hand away from her as she bolted for the door.

She took Callum's companions completely by surprise. Even as two dashed into the room to come to their leader's assistance, Moira tripped one and slashed her piece of glass across the other's jacket before flipping out the door and slamming it behind her.

In the darkness, Callum and his companions all heard the door lock, but Callum hesitated only a moment before slamming the syringe he held into his own arm. He fell back, gasping, as the T4 dosage began to take effect.

In the meantime, Moira yelled for Violet to wake up, though she'd been expecting that her brother would be the one she'd have to awaken.

"Come on!" she screamed as she held off Callum's final companion, making full and desperate use of her piece of glass. The man happened to be the other "policeman," but Moira didn't care about that right now.

It wasn't every day that Officer Myers found himself facing a screaming, angry girl armed with broken glass, but he did his best to deal with the situation anyway. He didn't do too badly, either, and after about half a minute he had his gun out and pointed straight at Moira, ready and quite willing to shoot.

"Give up," he panted, and Moira dropped the glass, slowly raising her hands into the air.

The man stepped forward, smiling a hard, forced smile. Moira held her breath as he raised his aim to her forehead.

"Don't have a reason to keep you alive anymore," the officer shrugged, and tightened his trigger finger.

* * *

Conner had stopped running as he approached the house, in case there were guards posted, but when he heard a single, faint and yet distinct gunshot, he abandoned all caution. Yet the thought struck him that he might need the police.

His thoughts sped faster than lightning, and when he ran into his first, darkly-dressed opponent, Conner threw him down only after whipping his gun away. It took Conner three seconds to turn and fire at the gasoline tank of the police car in the driveway; then, leaping into the air to avoid the initial shock from the explosion, Conner charged into the building, his gun at the ready.

"Moira!" He screamed his sister's name as he followed the sound of more gunshots, down the stairs to the basement.

* * *

It was Moira's voice that jerked Violet back to reality.

Her eyes flew open, and the first thing she saw was Moira pinned against the far wall with her hands in the air, and one of the abductors standing in front of her, ready to shoot.

"Don't have a reason to keep you alive anymore," Violet heard the officer say, and in that moment, Violet found herself flying off the stretcher.

The policeman's shot went wide as Violet landed on his back, bringing him down to the ground. Though Violet was still groggy, she woke up soon enough as she and the man fought for supremacy. In the end, it was Violet who won, by slamming her opponent's head roughly against the floor, three times. His eyes rolled back, and he was out cold. Violet stood up slowly, wincing as she brushed her hands off. She paused as she noticed the sounds coming from the locked door for the first time.

"Is he—is he going to be okay?" Moira's voice was shaky.

Violet shrugged, without turning to look at the younger girl.

"What do *you* care?" she asked, beginning to take off her jacket. Her voice sounded angry, almost savage, to Moira. "He was going to shoot you."

"Where's Conner?" Moira went on, taking a step backwards. She was a bit startled to suddenly find herself in the company of Violet's rough, violent fighting attitude that had made the former Violet Army leader what she was. It was quite different from the young adult's usual careless, sarcastic temperament.

"He's on his way, or he'd better be." Violet tossed Moira her jacket. "Put that over your head, get out of here, and *don't* stop."

"But—"

"Just go!" Violet shouted at her, before turning to face the door that was beginning to shatter. Gunshots sounded on the other side, and Violet smiled tightly, cracking her knuckles as she waited.

Moira promptly gave into her instincts and fled, holding Violet's jacket over her head as she'd been instructed. But she'd hardly made it to the stairs before she ran straight into her brother. Moira nearly fell, but Conner caught her.

"Moira! There you are," he panted. "What about the M—"

"They failed," she wheezed once she could speak again.

Conner was already half-helping her, half-carrying her up the stairs. They dashed out of the house together, into the quickly darkening evening.

Moira's eyes nearly quit as they rounded a corner of the house and came upon the remnants of the police car, shooting flames to high heaven. Conner didn't appear concerned about the fire, but only about his sister.

"Are you sure you're alright?" he asked, finally stopping once they were a safe distance away. "It sounded bad in there—"

He broke off as shots flew by, and Moira screamed, jerking the jacket off her head.

"Moira!" Conner cried out. "You're not hit—"

"No, no, I'm not," Moira gasped, touching her forehead again and again, as if she couldn't believe it. "The jacket—"

"It's Vi's," Conner surmised, whipping out his own gun once more and shooting in the direction the shots had come from. Finally they stopped. The twins could hear the wailing of police sirens quickly approaching. They were safe.

Moira sank down to the ground, panting.

"You're sure you're not hurt?" Conner asked her anxiously. "What happened to your hand?"

"I cut it," Moira explained breathlessly. "It's fine. But Vi—"

"Needs help. *Might* need help," Conner corrected himself. He nodded a couple of times, then did his best to smile as he straightened. "I'll be right back, Moira."

* * *

It was only a matter of seconds before the door was broken through. Having armed herself with the gun Myers had been carrying, Violet dove straight into the fray with her usual, reckless impetuosity.

She had no trouble with Callum's two collaborators. Within sixty seconds, both of the men were either dazed or completely unconscious, despite the fact that the second one had managed to shoot Vi's now-unprotected upper arm. But Violet knew, as soon as she first exchanged blows with Callum himself, that she had run into trouble.

Both of them were already injured, but Callum now had T4 as well, *and* had had time to heal slightly. Violet rallied all her strength to hold back the much older man's initial haymakers, while her arm continued bleeding.

Still, she didn't panic. It was only a matter of time before even T4, trained Callum would grow tired, and Violet had no doubt but that she could easily take him out then, no matter how young she was. After all, she was the former Violet Army leader, wasn't she? Her training must far excel that of an intelligence officer. There was no way Callum even had a chance of beating her.

Then he shot her, twice, near her right shoulder. Violet wasn't used to fighting without her basic protective gear.

She fell back for a moment to try to recover, but that moment was all Callum needed. He kicked her off balance, and when she stumbled back and came to a stop against the wall, he flipped across the room and held his gun to her unprotected forehead.

Violet felt a strange dizziness that blurred even the pain, but she fought through it. "Give up, Ranvier," she managed to whisper. "This isn't going to help you now."

The man bit his lip. "So you remember me, Trinity Ryder."

"I don't go by that name anymore," Violet breathed, but Callum ignored her.

"Let me ask you something," he went on relentlessly. "Your father was a strong man. He had high ideals and was perfectly prepared to carry them out to make a better world. If he'd succeeded, there wouldn't even be any such thing as kidnapping today, for example. Why did you get in his way?"

"Don't talk about him to me!"

Violet tasted blood in her mouth as Callum's free fist found where the bullets had hit her. "Still just as cocky?" His eyes flashed dangerously. "You were just a spoiled brat. It was your father's only weakness that he thought so much of you. And look how you repaid him."

He scowled. "I don't care about the Whyte kids. But if it weren't for you, we would have won that war."

"What do you think you're going to do about it now?" Violet panted, her own purple eyes just as angry. "Start another war? You won't win. No one ever will. Because people aren't meant to be controlled!"

"Little snip. So that's your tune now. That's how you got off nearly scot-free while your father was gassed half a year ago!" Callum felt the trigger experimentally. "You don't even deserve to live. I'll be surprised if anyone cares to come to your funeral, traitor!"

"No!" a third voice rang out.

Startled, Violet looked up as Conner skidded to a halt some feet behind Callum, lifted his own gun, and shot, all as smoothly and suddenly as if it had all been reflex.

Callum seemed to shudder for a moment, and then slowly he began to fall forward, his gun dropping from his hand.

Violet stumbled out of the way, suddenly collapsing against the wall as weakness overwhelmed her again.

Shaking, she touched her hand gently to her chest, wincing at even the minimum of pain it caused her. Her hand came away bloody, and she shook her head, realizing that superhuman or not, she'd have to get some kind of surgery done to get the bullets out. Violet closed her eyes for a moment, then opened them to look at Conner.

He, too, had fallen to his knees, but not because of any visible injury. He'd dropped the gun, and now he held his eyes tightly shut as he rocked back and forth in seeming agony. Violet bit her lip.

"Conner?" she breathed, her eyes widening in surprise.

He opened his eyes then, and a single tear slid down his cheek. Violet stared in terrifying déjà-vu of the day Conner had shot his sister. The change was the same, and looking into his eyes again this time, Violet could see only a frightened, horrified, despairing boy, though this time Conner wasn't screaming.

Finally he lifted his eyes to look at Violet. "Again?" was all he managed to ask. "Did I just..."

Violet's face, too, was white. "Trooper, you...you saved my life again."

"Why is this happening?" Conner whispered, his face drawn and tight. "I didn't want..."

"I'm sorry." Violet felt her eyes watering. "This is all my fault. I'm sorry, Conner!"

She was disgusted with herself.

Disgusted with every bit of the training she'd once put "Trooper" through. Disgusted with the amount of killing she'd made him do, killing for which she was responsible but for which he suffered the trauma.

And now it was her fault that he was remembering it all.

Violet's eyes squeezed shut as she tried to keep from crying as well. She knew that from the beginning, this had all been her fault. Her father had told her so many times that he did what he did, for *her*.

It didn't matter that Violet had ended with turning the tables. Callum had been right—how did she think she could ever be accepted into society?

Worst of all, why did she keep trying to keep in contact with the very same people she'd hurt—no, with the person she'd hurt the most?

Why did she torture him in this way? How could she think, perhaps, she could ever deserve his friendship?

No, she was lying to herself, and to him.

She could do nothing to anyone around her—but hurt them.

Why was she even still in Annapolis?

* * *

"Violet. Vi." It was Conner's voice.

Where am I?

Violet opened her eyes to see Conner's face as he stared at her anxiously.

She was in a hospital bed, she realized. Hurting, and tired—but alive.

But there was one thought in her head.

I need to go home.

"You're awake?" Conner asked hesitantly.

"I'm sorry," Violet breathed as all the memories came crashing down on her. "I'm...sorry."

"There's nothing to be sorry for," Conner shook his head.

Violet shook her head, and she tried to sit up, but just then a nurse came over and held her down, gently yet firmly. "Not yet, Vi," Nina laughed.

"I'm fine," Violet insisted, sitting up in spite of both the nurse and the sudden wave of pain that cut through her. "No, Conner, I'm sorry. Where's Moira? Is she alright?"

"I'm great, thanks," Moira spoke up from where she'd been sitting against the wall, out of view from the bed. She leaned closer, handing Violet a neatly folded purple bundle. "Here's your jacket back. I guess we both needed it."

Violet kept shaking her head, staring at Conner. "I'm going to go home."

"Whoa, what?" Conner's eyes went blank. "But you..."

"I shouldn't be making you hurt people anymore." The words came out almost of their own accord. "I shouldn't be hurting *you* anymore!"

"Vi." Conner's voice was soothingly calm. "No, *I'm* the one who's sorry. I realized. There's a difference." Violet just kept staring, so Conner went on. "He was trying to kill you, Vi. And I—I was protecting you. And that's okay. It's different from—back then."

He swallowed. "I would've done it for Moira, too. I did, actually. I would've done it for anyone."

"I saw you," Violet shook her head. "That was...what I taught you. Instant." She bit her lip. "Without a moment for reflection."

"Then you taught me well." Conner smiled weakly. "It's okay, Vi."

"You can't keep telling me it's okay every time I hurt you," she insisted. "Because it's not. I'd rather not be around if I'm going to keep hurting you."

"Was that what you meant by 'going home'?" Conner asked. "But don't go. I mean, go if you want, but come back. Because we're friends, Vi. That's why I did it. Because that's what you meant about taking the law into your own hands to protect the people you love, isn't it?"

Slowly Violet smiled, an equally weak smile. "Friends?"

"More than friends, if you like," Conner shrugged. "Actually, my parents were wondering if you'd be interested in hanging out at our house more often. You'd be less lonely that way. They're extremely grateful to you for helping me save Moira."

But Violet shook her head once again. "Sorry, but I'm fine with being alone…" Gradually her purple eyes lit up. "For now. Because…I have a friend."

"More than a friend," Conner reminded her.

She laughed. "More than a friend, then."

51

Book Three: Unfinished Trooper

Annapolis, Maryland.

9 August 2046 A.D.

Whyte Home.

Thirteen-year-old Charles Whyte was standing in front of the mantel in his Aunt Moira's living room. It was covered in pictures...and almost every single one was of Charles's older brother Evolet, who was going away to college next year. While Evolet was obviously bigger than Charles and had thick, dark brown hair, Charles's hair was a very light blond, much like his father's. His eyes were dark blue, also much like his father's. It was agreed among all the Whytes that while Evolet looked the most like their mother, Charles was just like their father.

But Charles wasn't thinking much about that right now; he was remembering. Things hadn't gone too well between him and Evolet when they had first met, three years ago. But Charles was older now, and so was Evolet. Charles wondered sometimes if he'd lost the chance to become a part of something like what Evolet and Jasmine still were—inseparable and the best of friends. The closest relationship Charles had to any of his siblings was the condescendingly friendly attitude Alison had with him. But she was cold with everyone. Anyone who had met Jasmine and Alison for more than five minutes could hardly believe that the two were twins. And Charles was becoming a loner.

He stood there a moment or two longer, his hands twisting irresolutely in his pockets. Then he appeared to make a decision, and he straightened and began walking out of the living room, down the hall to his older brother's room. Evolet still lived with Moira, and Charles was over for a visit.

The teenager knocked on his older brother's door, and it was opened a moment later by Evolet himself, after some banging sounds that sounded suspiciously like Evolet had flipped himself across his bedroom to get the door. Evolet looked it, too; his hair was rumpled, his shirt untucked, and his shoes half untied. Charles tried in vain to repress a grin. Evolet and his room were usually meticulously clean, thanks to Moira Whyte's constant upbraiding and encouragement; but today, it appeared, was one of Evolet's less clean days. But it looked like he was working on a project, over which he had tossed a sheet just before opening the door. Charles's eyebrows went up slightly.

"'Sup, Charlie?" Evolet demanded of his younger brother, with that perpetual half-grin, half-smirk that was always on his face. As he spoke, he ran his hands through his hair in a typically Evolet gesture.

Charles twisted his fingers nervously in his pockets. "I was wondering if you wanted to go on a walk or something...?" he asked hopefully.

Evolet's purple eyes met his younger brother's dark blue ones, and his grin widened and lost some of the smirk. "Sure. Hang on," he added, grabbing his purple jacket from the door handle. He glanced towards his window to make sure it was open, and then stepped out of his room, locking the door behind him. Charles's eyebrows shot up.

"How are you going to get back in?" he wondered, knowing that the key to Evolet's bedroom was one of those long-lost memories from the older teenager's childhood.

"Through the window," Evolet winked, leading the way down the hall. He felt his pocket, making sure that his phone was in it. It was.

"What if Aunt Moira has to get in while we're gone?" Charles muttered to himself, following Evolet.

"If she gets desperate enough, she'll call," Evolet returned laughingly.

Charles stepped outside the front door and joined Evolet on the porch, closing the door behind them. He smiled irrepressibly. It was autumn, and getting slightly chilly: Charles's favorite type of weather.

He could hear Jasmine and Alison shouting at each other somewhere nearby, and for a moment he winced as Evolet burst into laughter. Charles was dimly afraid that Evolet would call to them to join the group. But somehow Evolet seemed to sense that Charles wanted some time for just the two of them, and he didn't shout to the twins. They probably wouldn't have heard him, anyway. Whatever they were arguing about, it was definitely occupying most of their attention.

"Well." Evolet fixed Charles with one of his keen, penetrating stares. "Where to?"

"I—I dunno," Charles admitted, stammering. "Nowhere."

"My favorite place." Evolet smirked suddenly. "Let's run, then."

And so they ran, down the street, past their obliviously distracted twin sisters, out of the suburbs, and into the heart of Annapolis. Evolet could run faster than his younger brother as a matter of course, but he liked to let his younger siblings keep up with or even run faster than him. But Charles realized that, and did his best to keep up.

"Where are we going?" Charles shouted into the wind as Evolet dodged a speeding vehicle in the nick of time, the driver of which honked annoyedly at him and slowed down considerably.

Evolet laughed recklessly. "Nowhere!" he shouted back in turn, and Charles had to smile. But a moment later Evolet had corrected himself. "How about the bridge?"

There were plenty of bridges, but Charles couldn't help but know which one Evolet was talking about—the one nearest to their house, one of Evolet's favorite places to hang out with anyone who wouldn't call him "crazy" for it—though everyone called him crazy for anything, anyway.

"Sounds good to me," Charles nodded, tearing along. It was his turn to dodge out of incoming traffic, but Charles caught his breath in surprise as Evolet grabbed his hand and helped to pull him out of the way. But Charles knew why.

He might be thirteen, but he was still considered the baby of the family. Charles told himself not to resent the measure Evolet had taken for his younger brother's safety, but he bit his lip anyway. He wasn't a baby anymore.

And then they were there. It would have taken anyone else at least fifteen minutes, but for two superhuman teenagers it was a matter of less than five.

Ignoring some unsuspecting pedestrian's warning, the two gradually lost themselves among the bridge's supports, ending up somewhere underneath the bridge itself, watching the sunset.

Charles felt slightly out of place himself, but he only had to glance at Evolet's face to see that the older boy was completely at home among the steel rods and ramps. Evolet chose an extremely precarious-looking position, sitting on a narrow beam and leaning against a larger support.

Letting a small smile play over his face, Charles found a somewhat safer spot and held on grimly, all the while retaining an expression of distracted nonchalance.

"What are we here for?" he wondered vaguely. He was facing away from Evolet; there was a large beam in between them, the one that Evolet was leaning on and playing rock-paper-scissors with himself.

Evolet clapped his hands together; the sound startled Charles and almost made him fall. "That's for you to answer," he replied thoughtfully. "What are we here for? Swimming?"

"Mom would kill me if I went home all wet," Charles laughed.

Evolet's purple eyes twinkled. "So what you wanted was an escort home?"

"No," Charles replied abruptly, scowling although Evolet couldn't see him. He stared away, into the sunset.

Evolet didn't press the question, and for a few moments they were silent. Below them flowed the waters of the Annapolis harbor; from above came the sounds of busy, "rush hour" traffic. The horizon was streaked with red, orange, and purple. Charles glanced down uneasily as a boat passed underneath them, but none of the occupants noticed the two teenage boys and their high perch.

"Isn't it beautiful?" Evolet breathed, still staring at the sunset. Charles nodded, half-smiling.

And suddenly the younger boy made up his mind to speak. "So you're leaving next week." He said it as more of a statement than a question.

"Yeah," Evolet nodded. "On Friday. In eight days."

"And then the girls and I will be starting school the next Tuesday," Charles went on. "Are you going to be coming back for a vacation anytime soon?"

Evolet shrugged, leaning back leisurely over the waters. "Probably at Thanksgiving. And then for Christmas and then for Easter, I'll bet. But we can talk on the phone."

"Yeah, I guess so," his younger brother admitted. He stared blankly at the water.

"Are you gonna miss me?" Evolet asked half-jokingly.

Charles bit his lip. "That's a secret," he returned carelessly. He didn't feel like admitting something like that to Evolet—Charles would never hear the end of it.

"You'll take care of Jaz and Ali for me while I'm gone, right?" Evolet questioned after a bit of an awkward pause. "Don't let them get into trouble."

Now Charles had to laugh. "I can't do anything," he retorted. "I'm the baby, you know."

"You're not a baby," Evolet returned with a vehemence that startled his younger brother. "You're just the youngest. What's wrong with that? Man, you're thirteen! You're a *teenager!*"

"Well, I still can't *do* anything," Charles shrugged, narrowing his eyes.

Evolet reached over dangerously to pat the thirteen-year-old's back. "Just be patient. You'll get the chance to prove yourself eventually. And when that chance comes, I want to be the first to hear about it, okay?"

* * *

Charles had taken his older brother's words to heart, but he wasn't thinking of them right now as he stared dully at the tiny, orange tabby kitten meowing plaintively as it brushed against his sneakers. Charles wondered if his parents would let him keep it if he took it home.

It was hungry and hurt, the boy knew. He had just rescued it from a couple of bored street kids who were determined to get all the fun they could out of the little animal—Charles hadn't had to resort to violence, being unusually persuasive and having had a couple of dollars in his pocket to present when one of his opponents claimed that the kitten was theirs. Charles had waited for the two to leave before putting the kitten back on the ground, stroking it awkwardly for a moment before trying to walk away.

That had been a couple of blocks ago. The kitten had followed him, meowing pitifully as it limped along. Charles didn't have the heart to make it keep walking, but he didn't know what to do with it if he picked it up. So now he stopped, pondering: *Is Mom gonna be annoyed if I take this thing home?*

It was going to follow him whatever he did now, he knew. Unless he broke speed and deserted it. The kitten was so hungry and hurt that it wouldn't be hard to lose in a race like that, but Charles didn't want to do that. He had never had much use for animals or pets, himself, but he couldn't just leave the kitten to die or get run over like that.

"I don't think Mom likes animals," he told the kitten finally, biting his lip as he crouched down closer to its level. Oblivious, the kitten ran over to him and began licking his hand again. Charles smiled in spite of himself, scratching the kitten under its chin; it purred contentedly.

"Well, I guess there's nothing for it, then," the boy decided finally—and sneezed violently. He started, as did the kitten, but then the boy shrugged helplessly and wrapped his arms around the kitten gingerly, trying not to hurt it. In return, the small animal meowed happily and tried to cling to the boy's bulletproof purple jacket—and failed. The kitten squealed confusedly.

"It's okay," Charles muttered, feeling another sneeze coming on. It was strange; he rarely sneezed. "I've got you."

Finally the kitten settled contentedly in his arms and fell asleep almost immediately. Charles set off for home, sneezing and wondering what on earth had gotten into him.

* * *

"What is that?" Violet Whyte demanded as soon as her youngest son stepped in the front door. "A...cat?"

"It's a kitten," Charles clarified—and abruptly sneezed.

Violet eyed both Charles and the kitten uncomprehendingly. "What's it doing here?"

"Some nasty kids were hurting it," Charles told her falteringly, "so I, uh, uh—!"

He sneezed again.

"Are you allergic?" Violet asked suspiciously. "If you are, I don't think we're keeping that animal anywhere near here."

Charles's eyes widened. "But, Mom—"

Her gaze softened. "I know you want to keep it. But you don't want to constantly feel sick for the next twenty years, do you?"

"I'll find someone else to take care of it, then, I guess," Charles sagged.

Violet smiled. "Good idea. And then you can probably visit it sometimes."

"How do I have allergies, though?" Charles muttered. "We're supposed to be superhuman, aren't we?"

"So we are," Violet laughed. "But...that doesn't make us less *human*. And I don't believe allergies has anything to do with what makes us different."

"Alright," Charles nodded—and sneezed again.

"You can get a box for it in the garage," Violet pointed as she continued on her way to the laundry room. "Ask one of your sisters to feed it. And then you can figure out what to do with it tomorrow."

"I suppose so." Charles headed back out the door, towards the garage.

"Welcome home, by the way," Violet called after him.

Charles smiled vaguely. "Thanks. You too, Mom!"

* * *

"Let's see...who would possibly want you?" Charles wondered aloud to the cat the next day, his face perplexed as he gingerly stroked the kitten's tabby-orange fur. "Not old Mrs. Jeanie down the street—she's got a houseful of cats already. Jaz wants you, but Mom says she can't have you because I'm allergic. I wonder if Aunt Moira would take you...but I go over there all the time, so that might not be a good place either."

The thirteen-year-old sighed.

"Any ideas?"

The kitten purred, rubbing its tiny head against his hand and licking his fingers. Charles sighed.

"That's not helpful," he muttered. "Okay, then. I guess we'll just go scout out the area together."

* * *

Charles knew the truck was coming, at least twenty seconds before it hit him. He just didn't think it would actually hit him. Yet he distinctly remembered holding the kitten's box more tightly against his stomach to shield the young creature, while wondering vaguely if it was worth his time to get out of the way.

Then it hit him, knocking him flying into the pavement directly in front of the truck. Charles's sharp reflexes helped him keep rolling, away from the incoming tires, and his arms formed a cage around the kitten's box in a desperate attempt not to crush it. He finally lay still a few inches away from where the truck stopped, breathing hard and slowly letting all his muscles relax.

He heard the car door swing open, followed by someone's quick footsteps as they came around to see the kid they'd hit. But Charles smiled as the kitten crawled out of the demolished box, onto his face, and meowed plaintively at him.

"You okay, kid?" The driver bent down, looking anxiously at Charles's face. Slowly Charles nodded. "Yeah. I'm fine."

"But I hit you, didn't I?"

The man's hands were shaky, Charles noticed. He realized the man was probably more shaken than Charles himself was. He reached out to take the man's outstretched hand and stand up—and immediately fell back again as the driver slammed a needle into Charles's arm.

"Hey—" Charles yanked his arm away. "What are you doing?"

The man gave answer by pulling out another needle, one that this time found its way into the side of the teenager's neck.

Charles kicked the man away and held his ground for a few seconds, but then he felt his senses fading. He stood up, ready to fight—and fell to his knees again with a vague sense of slow motion.

"You…" he muttered, just before everything finally went black.

* * *

The first thing he heard was a little boy's crying. Charles opened his eyes, vaguely annoyed that all he could see was darkness. A blindfold, he assumed.

"You alright?" he began to ask, but that was when he discovered he'd been gagged, too. Charles sighed irritatedly, testing the bonds that knotted his wrists together and then his ankles. But they wouldn't loosen—or snap.

But the gag wasn't made out of the same material, Charles surmised. Resignedly he began trying to chew his way through the mass, and finally the shreds fell away. He could talk, though he couldn't see.

"Hi," he told whoever else was in the room. The sniffling subsided slowly.

"Are you—are you—" It was a little boy's voice; the kid couldn't be older than four or five, Charles decided.

"Yeah, I'm a friend," he assured the kid. "Are you okay? Can you see me?"

"I can see you," the boy replied slowly and carefully.

Charles smiled weakly. "Can you get this thing off my eyes, then, please? Or—"

"Okay," came the answer. There was some shuffling, and then Charles felt the cloth jerked away from his eyes. He opened them again, and this time he could see.

The boy was definitely less than half as old as Charles. He was leaning over Charles's face now, his little, chubby face anxious and scared. Somehow Charles twisted himself into a sitting position, his hands and feet still tied, and slumped against the concrete wall. The walls, floor, and ceiling were all made of the same cold, hard material, he noticed.

"Where are we?" he wondered thoughtfully, while mentally noting that the little boy didn't seem to have been restrained in the least, while Charles was held back by a material that had definitely been selected for strength and durability.

"I don't know," the boy told him tearfully. "They took me and I woke up here."

"Who? More than one?" Charles questioned.

"Three," the boy answered, after a moment's thought. He held up four fingers, and Charles nodded comprehensively.

"Mhm," he murmured, with a sideways glance at the room's wooden door. "Have they come in since?"

"Only when they put you here, too," the boy explained. "Then they leave again."

"I see." Charles glanced down at the material that held his ankles together, since he couldn't see his hands because they were behind his back.

"It's pink," the boy declared, seeing where Charles's attention was now concentrated.

"Purple, really, but pink works," Charles shrugged. "How long have you been here? Did they feed you?"

"No, and I'm starving!"

Charles smiled lightly as he glanced at the boy's chubby face; the boy most certainly was *not* starving, at least not in the literal sense of the word. "I'd say it's been a few hours, then."

"And I want my mommy!" Suddenly the boy burst into loud wailing, while kicking his feet against the floor.

"I—want—my—*mommy!*"

Charles winced, shutting his eyes tightly. "It's okay," he assured the child quickly. "We won't be in here for long—" He broke off as the door was suddenly flung open.

"Shut up!" a man whom Charles hadn't seen before yelled at the younger child, his face hard and angry.

"He wants his mommy," Charles spoke up needlessly, watching the man carefully out of half-closed eyes.

The man stepped closer to him, his face livid. Clearly his day was not going well.

"I don't give two cents if he wants his mommy," he growled. "All I want is for both of you to shut up. Now. Or I'll shut you up."

"I want my mommy too—" Charles began. The words were cut short as the short-tempered kidnapper used his boot to shove Charles's head hard towards the concrete wall.

"I said shut up," he hissed in the boy's face as he whipped out a replacement gag from his pocket. "Or I'll—you little—!"

Charles kicked him again, this time in the stomach. Staggering back, the man dropped the gag and pulled out a knife as Charles clenched his jaw and held his feet straight out, up towards the man.

"Give up, kid!" the man yelled.

"Change that to Trooper, if you don't mind." Charles grunted as he lunged forward anyway, catching the blade in between his ankles, just in the right place to both cut through his bonds and pull the knife away.

While the four-year-old onlooker gasped in amazement and shock, Charles flipped himself onto his feet, throwing his body at the man before he could react. Two swift headbutts to the chin took the kidnapper out, and Charles backed up towards the wall, breathing heavily. His hands were still tied, but somehow he kept his balance as the man crumpled to the ground.

"Let's get out of here, kiddo." Charles winked at the four-year-old—then jumped violently as there was a gunshot in the hallway. A bullet tore into the room, just barely missing Charles.

"Yah, they mean *business!*" Charles shouted, half to himself, as he flipped his way across the room, forgetting about freeing his hands. "Get that guy's phone out of his pocket, kiddo, and call the cops!"

He swung himself out into the hallway. Another bullet hit him squarely in the chest—or it would've if the purple material of the boy's jacket hadn't been in between.

The second man didn't have a chance to shoot again before Charles knocked his gun away and had him on the ground, with Charles falling forward onto the man's stomach, unable to stop himself without the use of his hands. That winded the kidnapper, and Charles was quick to take advantage of that fact to knock him unconscious as well.

"Alright," he panted, "that's two. One more—or possibly two more. Eh?"

"Give up," someone gritted. Charles held his breath as the end of a gun was pressed to the back of his head. "Give up, superhuman kid, or I'll prove to you that you're part human after all."

* * *

"Yeah, um, we were kidnapped," Charles was saying into the phone fifteen minutes later. "The address? Oh, I don't know, but—"

"Are you okay!" Charles could tell that his mother was throwing on her jacket; her voice sounded a bit distant, then came back again as she picked up her phone once more. "How did you get kidnapped! I'm on my way! Where are you? Is anyone with you?"

"It's nothing, I think," Charles replied slowly, trying to think of how he could possibly calm her down. "Um, Mom, actually—"

"If they catch you on the phone, give them everything you've got! I trust you, Charlie! I'll be right there!"

Charles eyed the three prostrate forms of the kidnappers on the floor. "I think I'll be okay, Mom. You see—"

"You don't have any idea where you are?"

"I can find out, but—"

"Are you sure you're not hurt?"

"Mom!" Charles almost screamed. "Can I please—just—really quick—say something—"

"What is it?" Violet demanded. "Are you okay?"

The thirteen-year-old cleared his throat. "I'm fine, Mom. The kidnappers are on the floor, okay? They're out. They're unconscious. They're... Anyway, we're free."

"Why didn't you say so?" Violet sounded exasperated. "Who's 'we'?"

"Me and some other kid." Charles was relieved that he'd finally gotten his message across. "I think they wanted him for ransom."

"And you?" Violet wondered.

Charles bit his lip. "I don't know what they wanted with me, but they sure didn't get it, that's for sure."

"Alright." Even through his mother's voice, Charles heard the distant sound of the car's engine being started. "Go find out where you are, then tell me. Your brother and I will be *right* there!"

* * *

"Kidnapped!" Evolet exclaimed as he dashed into the room ahead of his mother. "You little sneak, why'd you have to wait until you were by yourself? Lucky snip!"

"Kidnapping is no joke," Violet frowned, yet she breathed a sigh of relief as she saw her youngest son, safe and sound. "Thank goodness you're alright. Who'd you rescue?"

"Me, rescue?" Charles echoed in disbelief. He gestured toward his new friend, the four-year-old who now stood shyly against the wall, watching Violet and Evolet warily. "No, he did it all! Didn't you, Johnny?"

The four-year-old shook his head emphatically, making Evolet laugh heartily.

"His name is Johnny?" Violet raised her eyebrows.

"No," Charles admitted. "I don't know what it is. But we can probably find that out easily, can't we?"

"I suppose so," Violet agreed. She held out her hands, smiling amiably at the little boy. "Want to come with us, eh? We're friends!"

But the four-year-old squealed, running straight to Charles, who sighed. "It's alright—he can come with me. Where are we going first?"

"Police station," Violet supplied. Her purple eyes laughed as she saw the way the four-year-old implicitly trusted his superhuman rescuer. Oh, for the innocence of childhood.

"Noo!" Evolet ran a hand through his hair annoyedly. "Why did I come? I'm so dead!"

"You don't have to come," Charles told him gravely. "You can look for my kitten. I have no idea what happened to it."

"Are you serious?" Evolet's purple eyes opened wide. "Look for a kitten? In a city like this?"

Charles shrugged. "You sort of offered. So, last place I saw her was three blocks west from our house. Good luck. Thanks, Evy." He smiled a bit smugly as he followed his mother out of the building, towards the car that was waiting outside.

"Don't forget to restrain those three for the police," Violet called over her shoulder. "*Mille grazie!*"

"Hang it." Evolet whistled softly as he was left alone in the building. "It's either police or cleanup!" Resignedly, he began looking for something to use to tie down the three men. "At least...at least cleanup doesn't talk, does it." He sighed as one of the men began to stir. "Or it'd *better* not!"

* * *

Hours later, Charles and Violet returned home, having reported to the police and been assured that the four-year-old's parents would be contacted. All was well that ended well—they were both agreed on that, though they were both equally tired.

And yet Evolet seemed to be more tired, judging from the fact that he'd apparently forgotten that he lived with Aunt Moira and was sitting on his parents' front porch, waiting for his mother and brother to return home.

"How were the police?" he asked, yawning as he stood up and bolted to open the door for his mother.

"Great." Charles flashed a grin. "I'm going to be famous!"

Evolet shook his head in disgust. "You think that's cool? You'll live to regret every time you make it into the newspapers, believe me!"

"You've only been in them for a week, and that was a few years ago," Violet reminded him thoughtfully, brushing by her eldest son as she entered the house. "Why are *you* here, anyway?"

"Well, Aunt Moira's here, as I found out when I came home to find all the doors—and windows—locked." Evolet scowled. "Even my room window," he added in a whisper to Charles, as the two boys followed Violet down the hallway into the main partition of the house.

"I thought you locked your room door," Charles murmured.

"I do, but I guess she has a key." Evolet sighed hopelessly. "I hope she didn't see it."

"See what?" The thirteen-year-old raised his eyebrows.

Evolet clapped his hand over his mouth. "Nothing. *It.*"

"You've got too many secrets for your own good." Charles elbowed his older brother jokingly.

"I probably do, eh." Evolet shoved back good-naturedly in return, sending his younger brother flying into the wall. "Oops. You okay?"

"You can't hit half as hard as those kidnappers could," Charles rolled his eyes. "Pathetic for a superhuman, if you ask me."

His brother smiled dangerously. "Nah, I'm just being nice."

Charles grinned. "One of these days we should really try to find out who's stronger. I'll win."

"You will," Evolet agreed, "because I'm too nice to let you lose. Like Jaz."

"I really *can* beat her!" Charles scowled, leaping ahead of his brother into the living room. "Oh—hi, Jaz. Hi, Ali. Hi, Dad."

"Hey, son." Conner Whyte smiled lightly. "Still in one piece, I see. You scared your mother and I to death earlier."

Charles glanced down at his shoes. "Sorry. But I wasn't *trying* to get kidnapped."

"Next time, leave the guns and knives for professionals." Finally Conner allowed his smile to overtake his face as he nodded in approval to his son. "But I say: Well done."

"Three cheers for Charlie!" The twins burst out of hiding, and Jasmine wrapped her arms around her little brother. "Cool, squirt."

"Let me go," he protested helplessly. "Okay. Thanks."

"Three cheers for Evy, too," Alison smirked. "He found your kitten, did you know that?"

"He did?" Charles stared at his older brother suspiciously. "What'd you do with the poor thing? I hate to think of your getting your paws on the creature."

"Me too," the twins chimed in agreement.

Evolet scratched his head, perplexed. "Well, have it your way. But I gave her to Dad, and Dad—"

"Needed tissues," Conner put in helpfully.

"So I took her back outside," Evolet grinned, "and headed off to find Aunt Moira, but Aunt Moira wasn't at home and I found out later she was on her way here actually, and I'd just missed her, so instead I asked Mrs. Jeanie if she wanted another cat, and the dear old lady said yes—"

"Oh, you—" Charles shrugged. "Well. Thanks anyway. Mission accomplished."

"Are you done talking yet?" Aunt Moira asked, popping her head out of the kitchen doorway. She looked vaguely amused, but also stressed. "And Evolet needs to review his grammar."

Evolet ducked under the sofa. "Yes, ma'am!"

"Get back out here," Moira Whyte scowled, pulling him out with no hesitation in the least. "Do you realize you're about to start college? You need to cure your habit of silliness!"

"Yes, Aunt Moira," the teenager conceded meekly, combing the cobwebs from his thick, dark brown hair. "Okay."

"Besides that, tonight's dinner is to celebrate—no, commemorate—" Conner didn't get any further.

"Definitely to celebrate," Jasmine grinned mischievously. "Good riddance, Evy!"

"Can you wait until I'm actually leaving?" Evolet sighed. "Otherwise I don't think you deserve what I made for you all."

"Leave him alone until tomorrow," Violet instructed calmly. "That's in... five hours and twenty-nine minutes." Smiling, she joined her husband on the sofa.

"Anyway, Evy, we made something for you, too," Jasmine put in eagerly, before glancing around the room. "Or at least, Livia and I did."

"Did you?" Evolet raised his eyebrows. "What, a time bomb?"

"Noo!" Jasmine scowled. "It's...this."

"*Trooper A+*," Evolet read the notebook's cover thoughtfully. "Ha. Ha. Ha. You're so funny."

Charles watched them almost wistfully as Evolet and the twins kept shooting humor darts back and forth, and the thirteen-year-old smiled to himself.

Three years ago he would've been fiercely jealous of his older brother. Maybe he was still, even now. But as he got older, he was beginning to appreciate Evolet's constant efforts to keep everyone around him amused, no matter what kind of situation they were in. Charles was beginning to appreciate that Evolet wasn't only a clown, he was also a tough older brother who'd risked his life three years ago to save the entire family. Yes, Evolet more than deserved all the attention he got. Charles was just proud to be his younger brother.

And yet, Charles wasn't going to leave it at that. Today was only the beginning. He was finally beginning to prove himself. In a way, he sensed that he'd still always be considered the "baby of the family" by his parents and siblings, but that didn't mean that he couldn't show he was worth something, too. He could be himself. Maybe someday he could even hope to match his older siblings. But either way, he'd always be there to back them up, and they'd do the same for him. Because that was what family was for, wasn't it? And no matter what happened, the Whytes would always stick together like glue.

Though maybe Evolet might end up driving them all crazy at some point.

"I need a grovel…givel…gravel…yes, a gravel," Evolet declared to them all. Suddenly sitting up, Charles realized he had no idea what the others had been talking about.

"What are you going to do with the gravel?" Alison asked seriously, while her twin sister coughed loudly.

"Well, hit it, obviously," Evolet muttered.

"That'll be fun," Jasmine remarked thoughtfully. "Okay, then."

"Are you *sure* you don't mean gavel?" Charles interrupted anxiously, while suddenly his two sisters half-glared at him, half-laughed.

"Gavel. That was it!" Evolet stood up suddenly. "Okay, I give up. Aunt Moira, can I have the house keys, please?"

"You sure you need those?" The woman raised her eyebrows sharply.

Evolet shrugged. "Not really, but you never exactly approved of my other methods of breaking in, so—"

"Alright, here they are, but bring them back safely." Moira tossed the aforementioned keys across the room to her nephew, who caught them easily and performed a neat, albeit desperate back flip in the process. "And you'd better be back for dinner. That leaves you with...seven and a half minutes," she finished, ducking into the kitchen to check the oven timer.

"Seven minutes, huh," Evolet murmured to himself. "Alright. I can do this!"

* * *

"It's a game," he declared to them six minutes later as he burst into the house panting like a dog, after a run that would've normally taken a car fifteen minutes. "We can play it...after dinner, I guess."

"What kind of game?" Alison wondered suspiciously.

"I don't know," the older teenager had to admit. "You'll have to judge for yourselves."

"How do we play it?" Charles asked interestedly. He'd never seen a game as big as the clumsily-wrapped package his brother was holding.

"We'll find that out after dinner," Violet announced suddenly, standing up abruptly. "Come on, kids. Leave that thing in here, Evolet, unless you want it to get dirty."

"Yes, Mom," Evolet nodded. He proceeded to glare at his siblings. "Come on, you guys, clear out—I've got to hide it!"

Finally everyone had made their way into the kitchen, and Conner led grace before they all sat down. It was a special meal for Evolet's last evening at home: one that both Violet and Moira had prepared together. Evolet would be leaving the next afternoon, so this was the last dinner he would have with his family for a while. The dinner itself was a combination of the much-beloved boy's favorite foods: *Jägerschnitzel*, macaroni and cheese, and chips with salsa. There was a lot of everything, and yet it all disappeared quickly, no unusual circumstance in a family full of superhuman children and adults who made it their business to be ravenously hungry for every meal. Then came dessert.

"Mint chocolate chip ice cream is the best," Evolet declared—needlessly, he thought.

"No, chocolate," Charles objected from the other end of the table.

"You two are boring," Alison yawned boredly. "I prefer rocky road, with chocolate sauce drizzled on top and crushed peanut butter candies dumped on top of that, all downed while sitting on the roof on a blistering summer's day. That's what you call worthy."

"I like chocolate trinity," Jasmine shrugged. "And you can't call that boring."

"Agreed," Violet spoke up amusedly. The daughter and mother winked at each other.

"Seriously?" Conner's eyebrows shot up. "I should've known. Okay, but my favorite is mint chocolate, too."

"What's yours, Aunt Moira?" Evolet grinned.

"I like all kinds," the woman shrugged. "Don't ask me to choose, or you'll have to buy me some of each flavor so I can taste-test."

"I think you like vanilla," the teenager went on regardlessly. "Or is that just because you're always on a diet?"

"I hope you have enough money for all that ice cream." Moira smiled contentedly. "I'll make an exception, for once, if necessary."

Evolet glanced up at the ceiling in calm despair. "Alright, I give up."

"Smart choice, son," Conner smiled, and Evolet laughed.

"Alright, I've finished," Violet announced suddenly. "Hurry up, all you slackers. I want to see what insane contraption Evy's coughed up now."

"Mo—om," the boy protested. "I only do things like this about six times a year."

"Yes, but when everyone's birthdays are close together, that adds up differently," Alison shrugged, standing up. "Alright, Mom. I've finished, too. Shall we go find out where he hid the bomb?"

"Sounds about right." Violet's smile widened as she joined her daughter *en route* to the sink.

Evolet stared in dismay at his half-finished bowl of ice cream. "Wait, don't touch it until I get there!"

* * *

"I feel like I've played this game before," Alison remarked thoughtfully, some fifteen minutes later. "That car trip across the country two years ago? But this is a physical version. I see."

"Pretty much," Evolet shrugged hopelessly. "You guys are too smart."

"If that's the case, then I can win this game the same way I won two years ago, right?" Jasmine reflected, a slow smile creeping across her face.

"No." Evolet smirked. "I dare you to try that again."

Jasmine stared at her brother for a moment, then laughed recklessly as she made a move. Evolet began to react, then started in dismay.

"But I—" The eldest broke off as Charles quietly put a piece onto the board.

"I win," the boy announced, laughing.

Charles grinned as Evolet's hand met his in a fist bump. "You sure do, Trooper!"

Book Four: Catch 22

Badrakh, Mongolia.
6 January 2052.
Whyte Home.

"I'm seriously considering shooting them, Scar," Evolet Whyte admitted to his wife. "Not now, of course. When they come to take us."

"And you really think they'll do such a thing?" Scarlet Whyte frowned briefly before turning to smile at their two-year-old daughter Via, who had just wrapped her arms around as much of her mother as she could reach and was blabbing about how she wanted a cup of juice.

Evolet sat down at the kitchen table with his cup of coffee. His face, usually so cheerful and optimistic, was lined with worry. He was tired from almost constant meetings with WIPA officials and even more constant discussions with his father and aunt about how to deal with the situation. The WIPA had only recently come into existence, but they had already started their self-imposed work of reforming society, and that included containing all superhumans—who had barely survived the incident with Eternity Labs and were now widely considered dangerous. And the government was supporting the movement.

"I heard today they're building a camp in Antarctica," Evolet told Scarlet suddenly. "And whom would it be for, but us? I think this is the kind of thing Mom saw coming."

Stirring a pan of chicken fried rice at the stove, Scarlet raised her eyebrows. "The whole idea of a camp is drastic. And it's also just a rumor."

"I have reliable sources, though," Evolet protested, sighing.

He managed a half-smile as little Via suddenly decided to recognize his existence and came running over, squealing happily, to try to climb into his lap.

"You see, Scar, that's a big part of their plans. They want to get rid of us superhumans, since we pose a threat to their one-world dominance. But they can't just wipe us out without sufficient motive, or no one will accept them."

"Well, shooting them would give them sufficient motive, wouldn't it?" Scarlet raised her eyebrows. "And for the hundred millionth time, my name is not Scar."

"Yes, but, we can't just let them do this to us," Evolet protested.

"Then we won't," Scarlet returned calmly. "What makes you think they even have a chance? You've been getting too stressed out about everything, Evolet Whyte."

Her husband sighed, pulling Via into his lap. "So you think we should run. Haven't we done enough of that?"

"I don't see why you're so worried about it, anyway," Scarlet shrugged. "Those world-wide organizations never work. And how do you think anyone is going to get us into a camp, eh?"

"That's what they're going to tell us today, I guess." Evolet smiled distractedly as Via stood up in his lap and threw her arms around his neck, hugging him with toddler-superhuman strength.

"What?" Scarlet's eyebrows shot up.

"An official or so are coming over for dinner," Evolet admitted slowly.

"And when were you going to tell me that?" his young wife demanded, suddenly glancing at the pan and wondering if there was enough rice there for five people. Maybe she'd have to make a side dish or two. It would be healthier that way, anyway, she reflected.

"I dunno," Evolet mumbled unhappily. "When you were in a good mood, I guess. But that's done now. Via!" he exclaimed suddenly, and the toddler shrieked in excitement at being finally noticed. Her father stared blankly at her. "Are your eyes purple, or are they blue?"

"Boo!" she shouted back conversationally. Evolet grinned and brushed the little girl's red hair out of her face. She caught her father's hand and held it tightly, so tightly that anyone but a superhuman adult would have winced. But Evolet just grinned harder.

"When are they coming?" Scarlet asked resignedly, dashing into the pantry to look for some kind of side dish. She emerged some moments later with a bag of frozen cheesy bread sticks.

"Any minute now," Evolet told her, then glanced down at their little girl, who was now exploring his lap. "No, don't touch that," he muttered to her, clapping his hand over his pocket. The toddler squealed in protest.

Scarlet had heard him. "Touch what?" she asked distractedly. "If they're coming any minute now, then perhaps you should set the table, eh?"

"As you wish," Evolet acceded graciously, gently depositing Via on the ground and standing up. "Five places?"

"Well, if there are two of them coming, I suppose so." Scarlet laughed shortly. "I wonder how many families have WIPA officers over for dinner?"

"Let's hope it doesn't happen again," Evolet murmured, collecting five plates from the cupboard: four ceramic, and one plastic for the toddler.

About ten minutes later, the table was set. It was nearly six o'clock, and the fact that the WIPA officials would definitely be arriving soon was made apparent by Evolet's constantly and nervously checking his watch. Scarlet took Via to wash up, and Evolet was alone in the kitchen when the doorbell rang.

His right hand immediately went to his pocket, the pocket Via had been trying to get into. Swiftly, Evolet called a warning to Scarlet and went to get the door.

The first officer was the one Evolet had been talking to recently, and he contented himself with shaking the young adult's hand. "Good to see you again, Mr. Whyte," he greeted him, in a very distinct British accent.

"You, too, Colonel Pekar," Evolet returned politely, though somewhat frigidly.

The second WIPA, whom Evolet hadn't met before, was a subordinate officer: a woman probably only slightly older than Scarlet, with crisply cut blond hair and sharp green eyes. She had a British accent as well, which Evolet noticed when she introduced herself as Joselyn Grey.

"Pleased to meet you, —Miss?" Evolet asked, and was reassured by her nod. "Miss Grey. Follow me, please, will you?"

He shook her hand as well, and then replaced his own right hand in his pocket, leading the way down the bit of a hallway towards the kitchen. Evolet invited his two guests to take seats; in the meantime, Scarlet and Via joined them. Evolet lifted Via onto her seat—despite vehement protests from the toddler that she could sit down without help—and then Scarlet brought the dishes of food to the table. Having introduced the two other Whytes to the WIPA, Evolet stood up to lead grace, and after a moment of hesitation, the two WIPA followed suit.

He was just about to begin with making the Sign of the Cross when there came the sound of an explosion from outside. The two WIPA glanced at each other; then Colonel Pekar began heading for the door. But Scarlet and Evolet beat him to it. The colonel had to be content with following the two superhuman adults, while Via scrambled down from her chair and tore after the three. Miss Grey stayed behind a moment, and if anyone had been watching her, they might have been surprised to see that she quickly emptied some packets of a white powder into Scarlet's, Evolet's, and Via's cups, before dropping the wrappers into the trash and quickly following the others to the front doorway.

There was a small blackened area on the driveway where apparently a small explosive had gone off, and nearby it was a message scrawled on chalk. *Get lost!*

Evolet took a picture of the message, his face contorting in anger as he did so. He wasn't going to try to look for whoever had done it. But lately, as more and more of their neighbors became suspicious and wary of them, even to the point of threatening them—anonymously, of course, for who wanted to publicly challenge a superhuman family?—he found himself having some of what he assumed were the same feelings his parents had had when he was little. This was a world that hated superhumans. Especially now, what with the WIPA propaganda.

"Rats," Scarlet muttered to herself as she, too, read the message. Then she turned as Via came tearing out the door, and snatched up her two-year-old before Via could get near the words, though obviously the child couldn't read yet.

"Mama what boom?" Via demanded enthusiastically, wriggling in her mother's grip so wildly that it would have taken a superhuman adult to deal with her, a task which Scarlet managed with ease.

"Don't worry about it," the older redhead shrugged. Her eyes narrowed as she looked up and saw the two WIPA standing in the doorway. Of course their relations were very formal and polite at the moment, but Scarlet knew that WIPA was behind a good deal of the anti-superhuman feeling.

"It's going to be fine," Evolet whispered to her as they both walked quickly back into the house, following the WIPA into the dining room. Colonel Pekar asked Evolet briefly what had happened, but Evolet's answer, though vague, was solid enough to make the colonel decide that perhaps minding his own business was a better plan of action. So Evolet led Grace—without interruption, this time—and the meal began.

The beginning conversation was friendly enough, as well as completely off-topic from the real reason the WIPA were visiting: they began with simple, normal chit-chat about the weather, everyone's well-being, and so forth. But much to Evolet's relief and Scarlet's annoyance, the conversation soon took a more serious turn. Via, who had done a good deal of giggling at the beginning of the meal, soon fell quiet, watching her parents and the two grave-looking officials. The tension built, and relations grew more and more tight as Evolet brought up the rumors about the camp in Antarctica.

"It's been tested and certified to be superhuman safe," Colonel Pekar told the young man, with the air of a proud engineer. "Of course, we haven't got a use for it yet, but—"

"Then why build it?" Evolet demanded, ignoring the fact that he was interrupting. "There may be a good deal of hostile public feeling towards us, but we haven't done anything."

The colonel shrugged. "Better to be safe than sorry," he countered. "Besides, if it is superhumanly safe, then it is doubly safe for non-superhumans."

Evolet sighed with his usual tactlessness, which nearly always came into play when he was dealing with those he knew to be enemies. "I was talking to Dad the other day and he said he'd been offered a tour. Uncle Jason, too."

"So they have," Colonel Pekar smiled. "That's why we're here today. We're hoping you'll come along for the tour. How about it?"

"You could've just sent me an email about that, you know," Evolet returned rather crisply. He'd stopped eating a while ago, and now his right hand went into his pocket again.

In the meantime, Scarlet's eyebrows went up even higher as she watched the conversation gain momentum. She hadn't really felt like joining in, and right now she was slightly more preoccupied in studying Miss Grey, who was also sitting out the talk between the two men. Miss Grey seemed to be watching two-year-old Via, a slight smile played over the officer's face. Normally Scarlet might have taken the interest to mean that Via was a cute little girl—though Scarlet didn't need any convincing—and she would've dismissed it happily. But coming from a WIPA...

"You did invite us," Colonel Pekar told him smilingly, and Evolet bit back the retort that it was a forced invitation if anything.

"You didn't tell me about this 'tour,' Evolet," Scarlet noted thoughtfully. "Via and I aren't coming, are we?"

"I don't thi—" Evolet began, but this time it was the colonel's turn to interrupt.

He did so without changing his softly smug expression. "But Mrs. Whyte, you'll be busy somewhere else, won't you?"

Scarlet was somewhat startled at being directly addressed by a WIPA for the first time, and she glanced at him blankly. "You mean with Via? But if she comes—"

"Oh, then you haven't seen it yet, have you," the Colonel "realized," though it was only too obvious to the Whytes that he had been keeping whatever "it" was from them. "Do you have the paper, Joselyn?"

"Yes," the British WIPA murmured briefly, taking her gaze off Via long enough to pull a medical-sized paper out of her purse.

The colonel placed it on the table between Evolet and Scarlet, and the two superhumans leaned over to read it.

It was about Scarlet, and her first reaction would have been to scream in laughter, had it not been for the generally serious atmosphere. It was a medical document, and one certifying that Scarlet Dawes Whyte was officially and dangerously insane.

Scarlet scanned it once or twice, then glanced up at Evolet, barely managing to restrain her hilarity.

He seemed to be fighting with the same emotion. "Where'd you print this off?" he asked, his voice dangerously close to laughter. "No one could be around Scarlet for more than two minutes and still think she's insane."

The same smile was still on the colonel's face, much to Evolet's annoyance. "You should be thankful, really, since you lost your case."

"What case?" Scarlet's eyebrows shot up.

"You know that it's illegal to inject yourself with a strain of T4 in the United States, don't you?" Joselyn questioned softly, and Scarlet glanced at her in surprise.

"That was an emergency. Everyone knows that. And besides, we aren't in the U.S. anymore. It's something on a national level."

"True, but we *are* the international police," the colonel returned. "And no one gets away with a felony like that. Of course, we do understand your situation. Why else do you think we bothered to get you a certificate of insanity? Insane people can't go to prison."

Scarlet caught her breath, but Evolet was already annoyedly refuting the colonel's argument.

"Scarlet's being crazy is a lie, and you know it." The young father slammed his fist on the table; dishes shook, and Via jumped. Scarlet put her arm across her little girl's shoulders, and Via giggled and hugged her back.

Evolet smiled for a moment. His little family was one he could kill himself fighting to protect.

But the colonel's expression didn't change, and Evolet's smile faded. "You can't do anything with that scrap of paper, anyway," he pointed out dryly. "No one's tried taking Scarlet to an asylum yet. And I'd like to see it happen!" he added, laughing tightly.

His left hand curled into a fist again, though his right hand stayed in his pocket. Things were going to reach a climax any minute now, and every one of the adults knew it.

"Well." Finally the colonel's facial expression fell into a frown. "Keep your eyes open, then."

He and Joselyn pulled arms at the same instant, though Evolet was only about one millisecond behind them. Evolet found himself aiming very precisely at the center of the colonel's forehead—only to discover that both WIPA were targeting—*Via*.

Evolet's expression hardened in surprise and then in disgust, while meanwhile Scarlet, who still had her arm around the little girl, glanced at Evolet.

A sharp command from the colonel forestalled Evolet's signal. "Away from her, Mrs. Whyte," he ordered curtly.

"This is unprofessional!" Evolet spluttered.

But Scarlet saw the cold gleam in both sets of WIPA eyes, and she knew that they would actually shoot Via if the young mother didn't listen. Yet she didn't; not right away.

"Mrs. Whyte," Joselyn warned her, a second or two later, while about six million possible reactions shuffled through Scarlet's head.

Via glanced at her. "Mama?" she whispered, and Scarlet smiled.

"Via," she murmured back. "It's going to be okay. And...sorry, Via."

Taking a deep breath, Scarlet shoved Via's chair back, hard, and stood up in the same motion. As the chair—and Via—clattered on the floor, Evolet stood up as well, his gun still in his hand. A moment later, he was surprised to find himself having to grasp the table in order to remain upright.

His gaze flew to Scarlet, who was in the same predicament. Evolet's jaw dropped as the truth hit him like a log over the head.

Drugs.

Via was still on the floor, wailing. She had screamed as she and the chair toppled over; normally it would have taken her about two seconds to be back on her feet, but something was different this time, Scarlet realized in horror. Via couldn't stand, either. Scarlet knew what she was feeling; it was as if her legs couldn't support her weight at all.

She held the edge of the table tightly, then had to sink back into her own seat, her freckled face quickly turning as white as both her surname and the streak in her hair.

She glanced at Via, then at Evolet, who had knocked his chair away when he stood up.

He couldn't sit back down, but neither could he keep standing and hold his gun at the same time. He chose to keep his gun; he sprawled on the floor and his chair some seconds later, yet valiantly kept his aim on the colonel.

Evolet was panting for breath, and Scarlet would have given almost anything to help him up, but she couldn't even help herself.

She bit her lip till it bled as Joselyn came around the table and pulled Via away from her fallen chair, towards the wall. The WIPA officer leaned the two-year-old against the wall, but kept a tight grip on her shoulder, and a moment later casually held her gun to the side of Via's head. Via squealed in protest, but Joselyn kept her there, and the two-year-old howled as her arm was twisted slightly. She stopped struggling.

Scarlet swallowed hard, staring at the gun actually touching her darling's bright red curls, but she was powerless to stop it. It was a horrible feeling, this helplessness.

In the meantime, the colonel came around the table and took the gun from Evolet, who didn't resist, knowing what the penalty would be if he did. Evolet had never wanted so badly to knock someone down before, but all he could do was accept the colonel's help back to his seat, this time farther away from Scarlet.

Sitting down again, he winced as he saw Via, and stared blankly at Scarlet, a kind of hopelessness in his purple eyes. Scarlet's blue eyes met his for a moment, but then she looked at the table, her heart pounding.

Somehow they had to rescue Via. Somehow... But how?

The colonel was smiling again, this time as he pulled out a slip of paper and put it on the table, along with a pen. "I'd like to get your signature on this, Mrs. Whyte," he announced shortly. "And then yours, Mr. Whyte."

Scarlet's vision was out of focus for a moment, but then she could see again, and she read the paper swiftly. It was a legal document, stating that she and her husband formally placed their daughter, Via Pacis Whyte, under her uncle's, David Dawes, Scarlet's brother's, and his wife Elizabeth Dawes's, guardianship.

There were reasons listed, starting with the fact that Via's mother was medically insane, but Scarlet didn't read those through. Her eyes blurred. So this was what they wanted.

Her fingers closed around the pen for a moment; then she dropped the writing implement, pushing the paper away. The colonel's eyebrows shot up, but Scarlet shook her head.

"I'm not signing anything until he does," she insisted, her voice wavery. Evolet looked up, and his eyes met hers again; he caught his breath as he saw that Scarlet was crying. But then he had to look at the paper as it was placed in front of him in turn.

His face turned a ghastly gray as he read it, and he glanced at Via again. Joselyn's face was tightly inexorable, and Evolet realized that it was either he sign or Via be shot.

He hesitated a moment longer. He had met David Dawes once, at Evolet's and Scarlet's wedding, in Germany. David and his wife Elizabeth had seemed a nice, normal couple. There was no real reason why Evolet hated to hand Via over to them, but for the fact that Via was a Whyte. She was his, and Scarlet's. *Theirs.* No one could change that. Of course he wanted Via to live a normal life, but—

And then Evolet realized, this same decision had been made before—by his own parents and about him. They hadn't been forced to give him up, but they had done it anyway, for his sake. They had loved him just as much as he and Scarlet loved Via. And yet...they had sacrificed themselves so Evolet could have a happy, normal childhood.

He knew why Scarlet was crying, and he also knew why she wanted him to make the decision. And to tell the truth, Evolet was surprised to find he even could make that decision. All he knew was that Via would be raised by Scarlet's relatives in Kansas, with her cousins. He had no way of knowing about the medication the WIPA would administer to the little girl to suppress her T4. Still less did he know that she would grow up not knowing him, rarely seeing her mother, and feeling horribly and terrifyingly alone and unwanted.

Memories of Evolet's own childhood with his aunt Moira came back to him, reassuring him. Besides, WIPA couldn't keep the family apart for long—and Scarlet and Evolet were signing the paper under force. They would see each other again soon.

Evolet ran his hand through his hair once, then picked up the pen. He closed his eyes for a moment, and then signed his name on the line, handing the paper and the pen back to the colonel, who gave them to Scarlet again.

She stared at her husband, agony in her blue eyes, and Evolet nodded, bowing his head. He could hear the scratching of the pen on the paper as Scarlet signed; the room was deathly quiet.

Scarlet's hand had never shaken so badly before, and she had to pause and steady herself before she could write.

Scarlet D. Whyte.

It was done. The colonel took the paper and the pen back, and Scarlet buried her face in her hands, on the table. Her shoulders shook as she began crying silently, miserably. She didn't trust herself to look at Via again, and so she merely listened as the colonel issued his instructions and Joselyn put her gun away to carry Via out to the WIPA's car.

Despite her resolution not to look up, Scarlet's emotions overwhelmed her again, and she looked up anyway as they took Via down the hallway and out the door. Via was looking back at her, crying and screaming, and their eyes met.

"Mama? Papa!" she wailed at the top of her lungs. "Mama—a!"

"Via," Scarlet whispered, and the word cut her like a knife.

Suddenly she couldn't take it anymore, and she stood up. For a moment, she stood; and then she fell, just as Evolet had. On the floor. And she couldn't get back up.

She didn't have any of Evolet's reassuring thoughts. All she knew was that they were taking Via and she couldn't stop them. She wished she hadn't signed; she wished she'd given in to her instincts and hadn't trusted the WIPA, not even for a moment. But it was too late now. Too late...

She could hear the colonel's voice as he talked to some of his confederates on the phone, telling them it was safe to come and pick up the two adults now, and that they "must be kept separated," but suddenly his voice was drowned out by a clatter as Evolet, too, left his chair, crawling underneath the table. A moment later Scarlet felt his hand in hers, and she opened her eyes.

Evolet was looking at her, his own eyes sad, but hopeful as well as he held her hand tightly.

"They can't keep us apart," he whispered to her. "Never. I promise. We'll find each other and be a family again, no matter what happens."

* * *

He felt so tired, and weak too—for the first time in what seemed like forever. But there was no pain, and the weakness gradually slipped away as he regained consciousness.

He could feel the pressure on his wrist now as someone felt for his pulse, and Evolet opened his eyes. Maybe he was surprised to find himself staring directly at his father, but his immediate worries were elsewhere as his memories flooded back to him and he sat bolt upright in the bed, slipping to his feet a moment later.

"Scarlet," he panted. "Scarlet! Where is Scarlet?"

Conner Whyte had been sitting in a chair next to Evolet's bed, but now he stood up as well. He had more than completely recovered from his dosage of Schwann3 some years back, but still his unwrinkled face was covered in worry.

"Calm down, Evolet. She's not here. They told me they were taking her to an asylum," he told Evolet slowly, watching his eldest son's face.

Even Conner winced as Evolet slammed his fist into the wall. "No," he breathed, "they can't. But we'll get out, and get her out, and rescue Via—where are we, Dad?" He looked at his father again, and Conner was relieved to see that he seemed to be regaining his normal composure.

"In their Antarctica camp," Conner told him simply, lowering his eyes. "Everyone's here. Well, mostly everyone."

"Everyone?" Evolet echoed, his eyes widening in surprise. "Why? How?"

"Michael and the other kids, Jason, Petyr, Flynn, and the twins. I don't

83

know where Joyce is. How'd they get you here? What happened to Via?"

"The WIPA have her," Evolet breathed, and suddenly he sat down again. "They tricked us. They say Scarlet's crazy. I have to go find her—"

Conner smiled slightly, tilting his head and glancing up at the ceiling where there was a small black camera. "It won't be that easy to get out of here, Evolet. Why do you think we're still here?"

"But we'll find a way—" Evolet began, then broke off, his purple eyes narrowing as Conner made a quick gesture.

"We could call 9-1-1 and tell them we've been kidnapped," Conner suggested gravely, and Evolet didn't even laugh. It wasn't funny. But he understood a moment later as his father went on: "That's a stupid idea, isn't it. But that's why I said it out loud."

Evolet bit his lip. So there was a microphone somewhere, and not just the camera. But there would probably be a penalty if he messed with those. And he didn't want to do anything that might have indirect consequences on his wife or daughter.

He stood up again, marching out of the room to inspect the rest of this so-called "camp." Conner followed him.

"I know how you feel, Evolet," he warned him quietly. "We both had family. And we both had to leave them behind. But then we were together again. Evolet... You're more reckless than I ever was, though. So watch yourself, because if you get hurt—" He paused for a moment, then went on. "If you get hurt, I don't want to have to face Scarlet when she finds out."

Evolet stopped walking briefly, and turned to smile at his father. It wasn't as carefree and optimistic as his usual smile; this time it was harder, like the smile of one accepting a challenge.

"I'll find a way back to them, Dad. And I won't get hurt."

* * *

Scarlet didn't know how she felt as she slowly took in her surroundings, listening to the WIPA officer talk. The panic she had felt before losing consciousness was gone.

She was sitting in a chair, her hands folded in her lap. The room she was in wasn't small, but it wasn't big, either; its walls and ceiling were white, and the floor was a cold, gray tile. The only other people in the room were the officer and a rather overweight woman whose garb proclaimed her to be a doctor.

Scarlet would have had no trouble getting out of a situation like that, but for the fact that the first thing the officer had told her was that her behavior determined how her daughter was treated. The threat had made Scarlet's blood boil for a moment and then almost freeze. They knew how to control her, didn't they.

"But not to worry, she'll be going to live with your brother's family soon, and we trust you will behave in order to keep things that way," the officer went on, with that mercilessly cold smile. "If you need anything, don't hesitate to ask. Any questions? Then I'll ask Doctor Hale here to give you a quick checkup."

"You can't do this, you know." Scarlet's voice was hesitant at first but then grew stronger as her sense of desperation revived her. "It's completely illegal, and if you WIPA have any sense of—"

The officer shook her head, still smiling. "That's alright, Mrs. Dawes—"

"What?" Scarlet's eyebrows shot up in spite of herself. "My name is not Dawes. What are you doing?"

"Oh, that was something I forgot to mention, I suppose," the officer realized. "Well, Mrs. Whyte. It's important that you understand that your daughter is going to be raised as Via Dawes, and if you want to see her again, you are in no way to mention the name Whyte. Is that clear?"

Scarlet hadn't realized she might be able to "see her again," but still she hesitated before replying. She couldn't just reject her name, could she?

"Understood," she said finally, and the officer nodded.

"Good, then. In that case, I will leave Doctor Hale to confirm your perfect health, and then I think it'll be time that dinner is served." Suddenly the officer's smile widened. "I trust you will enjoy your stay, Mrs. Whyte. Because it's going to be a long one. The water won't boil if you watch it, you know."

* * *

"She is in perfect physical condition, but you already knew that," Doctor Olive Hale was reporting to her WIPA superiors about half an hour later.

The doctor wasn't smiling, but the lieutenant she was making her report to wasn't looking at her. "Good," he commented shortly. "But you already knew where to file the information, didn't you?"

"Yes." It was clear from Olive's face that she had more to say, but the officer didn't notice.

"You may go do that, then."

It was more of an order than a permission, especially as the lieutenant was obviously busy, but Olive still hesitated. "Sir..."

"What is it?"

"There's something you ought to know." The doctor took a deep breath. "I don't believe Mrs. Whyte knows it herself yet. But..."

"But what?" the lieutenant snapped, finally looking up.

The doctor swallowed nervously. "There's another Whyte on the way, sir."

Whatever reaction she may have been expecting, it probably wasn't for the lieutenant to suddenly jump out of his chair, his face contorting in anger.

"What?" the WIPA officer spluttered. "You have to be wrong."

Olive merely shrugged. "Time will tell. I would say about seven months."

"Seven months," the lieutenant muttered to himself, writing a quick note. "I will have to bring it up to the Higher Council. Doctor Hale, I want you to keep me briefed on this, you understand? And remember, you're to begin Via Whyte's medical care next week."

"Right." Olive nodded. "Shall I go now, then?"

"You shall," the lieutenant agreed, saluting briefly as Olive left the room.

"Another Whyte?" he scowled to himself as he went back to his work. "The Council is not going to like this. But we'll have to get it away from Mrs. Whyte before we can get rid of it...unless the Council will want to keep it alive with the others. For a decade...or so..." He sighed. "Maybe we shouldn't be so socially conscious. But it doesn't matter, because everything will end the way it's supposed to, however long it takes."

* * *

By the time the "Higher Council" knew about the new Whyte on the way, so did Scarlet herself. She was happy, of course, but she didn't know what to think at first.

"If only Evolet were here," she whispered to herself one night. "He would be so happy. And Via. To think that she has a younger sibling and she doesn't know..."

She closed her eyes and sighed, remembering her little darling's many happy faces. Via wouldn't have understood her very well, but she would've been delighted anyway. But it was two weeks now since Scarlet had last seen her.

"Are you a boy or a girl?" she questioned aloud, and laughed. She was lonely, but she wasn't alone.

Scarlet was careful about what she ate now. She wouldn't put drugs past the WIPA, and she had been wary of what they served her from the beginning, but more especially now. The young mother was aware that they knew of the baby's existence, and she wasn't going to let them do anything about it. This young life was hers to protect, and Evolet's, and protect it she would.

"Forever," she murmured, but suddenly her face paled at the thought that they might try to take this child away, too. She knew she would be conscious to hear its first cries. She would be able to hold it immediately afterwards. The baby would be perfectly fine and healthy—hyper-T5 had stood both Scarlet and Via in good stead, and there was no reason it would be different for Via's younger sibling. But after that?

She was horribly afraid they would find some way to separate them, and that Scarlet wouldn't be able to resist. There was the thought at the back of her head that they would use Via to do that. But Scarlet didn't want to think about that now. She sang to the baby, and then as her voice cracked she hummed, rubbing the front of her yellow asylum dress. Scarlet hadn't bothered to tell them that she hated the color.

A memory came to her, of Evolet telling her that if they ever had a son, he wanted to name him Conner Aloysius, after Conner Whyte. And they would call him Aloysius. Scarlet swallowed hard, remembering, and a tear slid down her cheek.

"You'd better be a boy, then," she addressed the baby again, and laughed at herself, pushing her white-streaked red hair out of her eyes. "Because I won't know what to call you without Evolet, and I can't exactly make up a girl version of Conner, see?"

There was no answer. There couldn't be, seven months away. But that didn't matter to Scarlet, and she smiled fondly. When the time came...

"I hope this was the right choice," she whispered, this time to herself. "But raising a family was the best decision I ever made. Now all we have to do, little one, is get our family back together again. You'll help me, won't you?"

* * *

She would never forget the first time she saw the baby: a tiny, screaming little boy who was promptly weighed, measured, foot-printed, and blanketed by Doctor Hale before being handed to his mother.

Scarlet held him close, and gradually his newborn screams grew quiet. He wasn't quite as big as his older sister had been, but he was still bigger than the average baby. His eyes were, surprisingly, green. And his hair, much to Scarlet's delight, was a dark, curly brown that reminded her of Evolet's, though there wasn't much of it.

"How are you feeling?" Doctor Hale asked the mother.

Scarlet could see right through the fake smile, but she appreciated the gesture anyway.

"Perfectly fine," she replied truthfully. "I feel great."

"That's good." The doctor bunched up all the "biohazard" equipment she had used, and she promptly shoved it into the appropriate bin. She was about to do the same with the measuring tape, but Scarlet stopped her.

"No," she interrupted quickly, "can I have that? —Please?" Scarlet's freckled cheeks turned slightly pink.

It was a childish request, but Scarlet still had a childish part of her soul, and she had kept Via's measuring tape for that baby's scrapbook. She wanted to do the same for her first little boy.

Olive Hale's eyebrows went up, but she figured a short paper measuring tape couldn't hurt, and she gave it to her patient. Scarlet smiled gratefully. "Thank you."

"No worries," the doctor replied absently. "I'm going to be leaving now, Mrs. Whyte, but…"

"Yes?" Scarlet looked up from where she'd been folding the measuring tape at the same time as smiling for the hundredth time at the baby.

"There are going to be a couple of WIPA arriving soon, or so I hear," the doctor told her. "I just thought you'd want to know. And…" She took a deep breath, then went on without looking at Scarlet. "They'll be bringing Via."

Despite herself, Scarlet couldn't help smiling. It had been four months since she'd seen Via, and the little girl would be three now. Yet Scarlet had a feeling this was not a gracious WIPA condescension. There would be something to pay.

Doctor Hale didn't wait for a response before leaving the room; she closed the door behind her, and Scarlet and the baby were alone. It wasn't the first time, but it was the first time they'd seen each other, and just that in itself overwhelmed Scarlet. Life was such a miracle, especially this one. But all her fears were quickly coming back, and she began to wonder if this wasn't just her first, but her only chance to have him in her arms.

"Your name is Conner Aloysius Whyte," she whispered to him over and over. "Evolet Whyte is your father. I'm Scarlet Whyte and I'm your mother. You have an older sister, and her name is Via Pacis Whyte. I love you, Aloysius, and your sister loves you, and your father loves you too, even if he doesn't know you…yet…"

She sighed as her keen ears caught the first sounds of approaching footsteps in the nearby hallways. Aloysius Whyte whimpered.

"You'll never be truly alone, Aloysius," she told him. "I'll always be thinking of you…but please, will you remember me?"

Someone knocked, and then the door was opened. Scarlet glanced up to see two WIPA officers, one of whom was holding a little three-year-old, red-haired girl's hand. But when the girl saw Scarlet, the girl's face lit up and she jerked her hand out of the officer's, running to the bed.

"Mama!" she shouted; and then she stopped, staring with wide eyes at the bundle her mother was holding.

Scarlet's face was brimming with smiles. "It's your little brother, Via. Aloysius. Tell him hello!"

"Hello Aloyshus!" Via told the baby obediently. Aloysius stared rather blankly at her, and Via burst into giggles, looking back at her mother. "Mama he likes me!"

"I'm sure he does," Scarlet agreed happily. Yet a shadow fell over her face as one of the officers approached. Scarlet started as the expressionless WIPA took Via by the arm and pulled her rather roughly away.

"Leave her alone!" Scarlet shouted, ready to leap off the bed even while holding Aloysius—but a sudden gesture from the officer stopped her, as he pulled out a needle and held it firmly against the little girl's wrist.

"Now, this doesn't have to get ugly, Mrs. Whyte," the officer told the mother frankly, as Via fought and squealed. "You know what we're here for. I'd appreciate it if you'd hand her the baby," he added, gesturing to his confederate, who now came forward.

"Never," Scarlet hissed dangerously, her blue eyes narrowing into slits. "Why? And let Via go, or I'm not doing anything."

"No, no," the officer laughed. "That's not how it works. We need you to sign something."

"So you can take Aloysius away, too?" Scarlet's voice rose shrilly, in almost hysterical tones. "Why do you care whether I sign anything or not? If you can force me either way—and a forced signature means nothing—"

"I'm pretty sure your brother would appreciate legal guardianship," the officer shrugged. "Though, if you wish, we can take the little one into WIPA custody instead—"

"Just leave them with me!" Scarlet nearly screamed. "You have no right to them! I'm not crazy, and I don't know what excuse you're using to lock Evolet up, and I don't care, and—"

She broke off as the baby started crying, and stared at him for a moment before glancing back at Via. Scarlet was sitting up now, ready and on the alert, but she knew that if she did anything Via would be in danger. As if the little girl wasn't in danger already.

"Mrs. Whyte, please control yourself." The office shook his head, gesturing to his companion, who pulled out a small dart gun. "Watch what you say. And please, don't drop the baby. That would be sad."

Scarlet stared aghast as a moment later a dart hit her in the neck, and slowly she fell back, feeling her strength draining. The WIPA stepped in and took the baby, and Scarlet couldn't stop them. She bit her lip as something died inside her. This wasn't fair. This shouldn't be happening. Not again.

"See, it's not that hard," the officer went on, and Scarlet could have strangled him. "Though you could have made it easier. That's only going to last for a few minutes, though, and then you can sign this paper."

"I'm not signing anything until Evolet does," Scarlet bit out savagely.

The officer shook his head, smiling pityingly. "No, Mrs. Whyte—Mr. Whyte does not know about this child's existence, and he's not going to. This paper requires only your signature—and it'll have it."

Scarlet glanced over the paper, bravely resisting the urge to tear it to shreds. "This says Washington's going to take care of him," she realized, confused. Washington was her other brother, the middle child in the Dawes family. "Why?"

"David and Elizabeth Dawes have their hands full enough with their own children and this troublemaker here," the officer replied; and indeed Via looked the part, as she tugged and howled.

"Sign the paper, Mrs. Whyte. This needn't take all day."

The nightmare choice again. Scarlet's vision blanked temporarily, but they had the children, and she had no choice. But this time she had to make the decision.

She didn't see the paper as she signed it. Her eyes were full of tears.

"His name is Conner Aloysius," she told them as she did it. "Tell my brother. Tell him!"

They took the paper and left, ignoring her comment. But behind them, Scarlet clenched her fists together until they were white. She could hear her little boy crying, but the sound grew fainter and fainter.

It was too much. Who knew what would happen to Aloysius? Would they tell Scarlet's brother what to name the baby?

It had been a long time since she had seen Washington. What was he like now? Did he have a family?

Would Aloysius grow up with siblings? Would he remember Scarlet, or would he know even less about his parents than Via?

Why had WIPA taken her children away? Why had they had to take the family apart? How dare they touch her darling Via...and Aloysius... She could kill them with her bare hands.

Except she couldn't, because they held everyone she loved, hostage. She couldn't know them, she couldn't go to them. She couldn't help them. She had the measuring tape, but not...

The thoughts spun faster and faster, and Scarlet screamed, a piercing scream that was almost insane. But her stay at the asylum had only just begun...

Book Five: Like Water but Thicker

Location, date, and time Marked Classified.

How long will I be trapped here?

She knew where she was. She was strapped to a bed in some heavily guarded medical facility, just like she'd been for the last six weeks. Yet her existence had been, and still was, a hazy state of semi-reality.

She had blacked out when she hit the bridge. She could remember that much. But even when she'd come back to her senses, it wasn't complete. She was trapped in four walls, four clear walls through which she could hear the world around her. Four walls that held her prisoner.

She couldn't see, but she could hear. She could hear everything. People's voices. Sirens. Traffic sounds. And now, for the past six weeks, almost nothing but silence. She knew she was in a medically-induced coma, but she didn't know when it would end. *If* it would end. And now she was beginning to think that it wouldn't.

But today, Eryka Ulven knew that something was different. She felt restless. Almost as if the coma was leaving her. And gradually, she regained her senses.

It was her eyes that she could move first, and she did. She opened them and saw the room for the first time. It looked just as she'd imagined it. Blank, windowless, dark. Clean. Lonely.

Eryka turned her eyes towards the stand next to her hospital bed. She raised her eyebrows slightly as she saw that the supply of whatever had been IV-ed into her hand, had run out. Perhaps the reason for her coma? Or maybe, simply, life support. Either way, it had run out and Eryka was awake.

Slowly she regained control of her muscles, and Eryka tested her strength against the straps that held her nearly immovable. She accomplished nothing, and gave up after a couple of tries. There was no way she would've been left alone if she hadn't been adequately restrained.

She was surprised how refreshed she felt. Almost as if she'd been reborn. She could remember every bit of her brief terrorist war, but simply chose not to. She felt a strange resignation to her current situation. When Eryka thought about what she had done, she felt a strange, almost foreign horror. Maybe something like regret. But it felt like a bad dream.

But now Eryka looked up again as the door opened and a woman stepped into the room, walking slowly over to the lone hospital bed. The woman was dressed in full WIPA officer uniform; her hair was brown, and her eyes a dark gray. In her gloved hands, she held a syringe. The liquid inside was a tinted silver color.

Eryka followed the woman with her eyes, feeling horribly vulnerable as the officer stopped by the side of the bed. Eryka read the name on the woman's blood-splattered badge—Lieutenant Diana Anderson. But she didn't recognize either the face or the name.

"Do you remember me?" the WIPA officer asked, her face expressionless.

Eryka shook her head slowly, still staring intently at the woman. "No. I don't know you."

"You killed my sister," Diana went on, her voice cold and hard as she leaned closer. "You're the Wolf. You disrupted our entire program for global peace." Her face curved into a deep, dark scowl. "Do you remember *that*, at least?"

"Yes," Eryka answered simply.

Diana's eyes narrowed. "Good," she said, slipping the end of the syringe needle into the side of Eryka's neck.

Eryka didn't flinch. "Are you going to kill me now?" she asked, her voice quiet.

"No." Diana laughed, and Eryka's eyes widened in spite of herself. "No, Wolf... This is my revenge, Eryka Ulven. I'm going to turn you into the demon you tried to be!"

* * *

"Via? Hey, Via? You awake?"

Snapping out of her reverie, Via Pacis Whyte spun around to see her cousin, Julien Ransom, waving at her. Shaking her head quickly, Via straightened away from the porch railing and the words that had been scratched onto it.

"Yeah, yeah, I'm awake," she told her cousin quickly. "What?"

He shrugged, frowning. "I've just arrived for Christmas break and we haven't seen each other for about a month, that's all."

Julien looked her over. She wasn't much different from when he'd seen her last, except that her already-long red hair was about an inch or so longer. Julien remembered that Via had decided she wanted to grow her hair as long as her mother's—which was almost insanely long—and, so far, Via wasn't doing half bad.

"Oh, right." Via blinked a couple of times. "I forgot. Well, hello."

Julien stared her down curiously, then leaned forward to see what she'd been looking at. "What's wrong?"

"Nothing." Via's hand shot out to cover the words, but her cousin had already seen too much.

"The...Wolf?" His entire face contorted. "What's this?"

Sighing, Via let her cousin read the rest of the message. "It's just a threat, that's all." Turning, she began to head into the house. "Well, welcome back. I only got home three days ago, so..."

"You should tell your parents about the threat." Julien followed her, shaking his head in disbelief. "It doesn't even make sense."

Via paused in front of the door. "They already know," she murmured, and Julien leaned forward to hear her words. "This...is the twenty-ninth threat." Her scarred face was unexpectedly blank.

She pulled the door open and stepped inside. "Cousin Julien's here!"

Immediately the front room was crowded, first of all by two-year-old Stanislaus Whyte, then his younger sister Lily and their parents. Scarlet was holding Lily, so it was Evolet who shook hands with their nephew.

"Good to see you again," the adult grinned. "How's life?"

"It's okay," Julien began, obviously distracted. "What's up with the—" He broke short as Via's fist hit him squarely in the shoulder.

"What?" he demanded, irritated, but it was Evolet who answered the unfinished question.

"You know?" he asked, and Julien nodded. "Okay. We'll talk about it later, okay? Not in front of the kids."

Julien nodded silently, finding himself struggling to maintain balance as Stanislaus crashed into the older boy's lower legs. "Julie!"

"Julie's a girl's name," Julien complained, leaning down to grin at the boy face-to-face. "Call me…Jules. Can you say that, if you can't say Julien?"

"Juice," Stanislaus beamed.

Julien bit his lip. "Okay. Let's just forget it for now." Standing up, he glanced around. "Where's Aunt Jaz? Isn't she here yet?"

"Not yet, nor Grandpa and Aunt Moira," Scarlet shook her head. "But they'll be here tonight." She smiled. "Welcome home, Julien."

Julien smiled back, remembering that night a couple of years ago where the Wolf Pack had finally been defeated. When, in a way, he'd been accepted into the Whyte family…

Evolet's and Scarlet's house wasn't his "home," strictly speaking, but it still felt like one to Julien. Especially when his aunt was around, as she would be soon.

"Thanks." Julien nodded. "It's good to be back."

* * *

"What are all these about?" Jasmine was the first to ask, her face expression-less.

The two toddlers had finally been put to bed, and now the seven adults of the family were sitting around the dinner table, puzzling over the twenty-odd notes that had been collected. Every one of them was a threat. And every one of them was signed, *The Wolf.*

"Via started receiving them three weeks ago," Evolet explained quietly. "At college. And they've followed her here. In fact, the numbers have doubled in the last four days she's been here. Every time we step outside, there's something new."

"But people can't just leave notes," Moira shook her head. "You'd notice them."

Scarlet shrugged. "It depends how they leave it," she pointed out. "Some come by mail. Some by text. Some we just run into at the grocery store. The most unique one was on a toy arrow that was shot at Via when we were walking in the park." She frowned. "There were some kids nearby practicing archery. None of them looked suspicious. The only other adult around was just their second-grade teacher."

"Why are they all signed as if they were sent by Eryka Ulven?" Julien questioned confusedly. "I mean, she died in the explosion—"

"It's her handwriting," Via interrupted quietly. "Every signature is in Eryka's handwriting."

Everyone turned to glance at her. She was obviously the target of the threats, and it was understandable that she should look somewhat worried. Her eyes were strangely tired—Julien didn't remember them having been nearly as tired a month ago.

"But the explosion two years ago," Julien went on after a moment's pause. "That completely destroyed the entire building she'd been in. The former WIPA base. Remember? She was in a coma there. And then the place was broken into and completely blown to the ground by some group that thought they'd take the law into their own hands." He scowled. "Not saying I don't sympathize."

"We know," Evolet nodded, leaning forward slightly. "But the real question is: was it *that* group that set off the bombs? Or...someone else?"

"Eryka couldn't have," Conner mused, speaking up for the first time. "How *could* she? She had been in a coma the entire time."

"Or that's what we've been told," Scarlet nodded. "Well. That's what we've asked the police to look into. But we suspect that if the government is hiding the fact that the Wolf is on the loose somewhere, they won't tell us anything."

"So what are we doing about it?" Jasmine asked quietly.

"Nothing yet." Evolet stood up and began to re-collect the notes into the plastic bag they'd been kept in. "We just thought we'd make you aware of the situation. Just forget about it for Christmas, please." He smiled at his eldest daughter. "No one is going to hurt our Via."

"Right," Julien laughed. "You've got a whole team of bodyguards now, Via!"

The nineteen-year-old redhead laughed. "Sounds like a plan!"

* * *

"Why does your dad seem so unconcerned?" Julien asked Via later that night.

They'd both had the same genius idea of sitting out on the roof to stare quietly up at the stars, but that idea had been shattered when they had began talking. Down below, the New York City suburb life went on as it usually did at 2 AM; but on top of the two-story house, things were relatively peaceful.

Via shrugged. "Don't worry about it. He's got it under control."

"Well, I hope he isn't seriously relying on the police," Julien muttered.

Via eyed him annoyedly. "I said don't worry about it," she scowled. "It'll be alright."

Obediently, Julien changed the topic. "Well, two days till Christmas, huh," he murmured. "I love how cold it is out here."

"Me, too," Via agreed. She closed her eyes.

"Are you going to cut your hair for Christmas?" Julien wondered randomly. "It's pretty long. Past your waist."

The girl shrugged. "I don't know. Should I?"

"Hmm...yes," her cousin decided after a few moments of thought.

Via laughed. "Well, I'm not going to. Mom's is still longer."

"Aunt Scarlet has had years," Julien shrugged. "You'll never catch up."

"We'll see," Via laughed. Suddenly her eyes flew open as she sat up quickly. "Is it starting to snow?"

"It is," Julien laughed. "Awesome. Should we go back inside?"

Via's blue-purple eyes were riveted to the sky. "You can—I don't care. Oh wow. It'd better snow for Christmas day!"

* * *

Just as they had the year before, the family went to midnight Mass at the nearby church, while Moira generously volunteered to stay home and watch the toddlers. Everyone else hoped to sleep in the next morning...which was why Via was annoyed to find herself awake at 6 AM, only four and a half hours after returning home. But the lure of Christmas day proved too much, and eventually the nineteen-year-old snuck downstairs after changing into the new day's clothes and doing her long hair up in a bun.

As she'd suspected, no one else was even remotely awake, not even Moira, who planned to go to the 7:30 Mass. Sighing, Via headed for the coffee maker, then abruptly changed her mind and went to the cabinet for a packet of tea.

A few minutes later, she sat at the table by the window, messing with her phone and occasionally glancing out the window to see how light the sky was getting. About halfway through her cup of tea, however, Via stood up abruptly, staring even harder out the window. Apparently she'd seen something outside that had captured her attention, for the next few seconds found her pulling on her boots and heading outside into the fresh snow.

It was Julien who came into the kitchen next, about fifteen minutes later. Nothing seemed out of place to him, and he went right to making his own cup of coffee. After a secret peek at the stockings hanging over the fireplace in the living room, he sat down sleepily at the table for his daily caffeine intake—and noticed the half-finished cup of tea for the first time.

It was a small, plain white china mug. Julien stared at it for a moment before glancing outside. No one was within view, but Julien looked at the shoe-shelf anyway. He raised one eyebrow slightly, then back at the cup of tea as suddenly all the sleepiness disappeared from his deep blue eyes.

"Via?" he asked softly, but no one answered.

"You're not going to scare me," the twenty-year-old went on, carefully glancing around the room once more. "No matter how you sneak up on me, you're not going to—"

He broke off suddenly, his own drink forgotten as he stood up and quickly dipped his index finger into the cup of tea.

It was cold.

Without pushing his chair back in, Julien headed for the stairs, almost running into Moira the moment he stepped out of the kitchen.

"Have you seen Via?" he asked her quickly.

"Shh!" Moira held up a finger. "You'll wake up the kids!"

"Via's missing," Julien went on, dropping his voice to a cautious whisper.

"Via is...what?" Moira's eyebrows shot up.

* * *

Five minutes later, Scarlet and Evolet had been called to the kitchen as well; a quick search around the property had proved fruitless. The adults discussed the problem in loud whispers, but Moira kept glancing at the clock. Finally she stood up.

"I'm on my way to Mass," she announced. "I'll just say one thing. Start looking for Via now. Don't wait for the police. And don't even bother to contact them for twenty-four hours. If at all. They're not going to help."

With that, she was gone. Julien stood up, aghast.

"What are we going to do?" he asked Evolet and Scarlet, almost too loudly. "We can't just—"

"We're not," Evolet interrupted, suddenly looking up from his phone for probably the first time in five minutes.

He glanced at Scarlet and nodded. "He got it."

"Who got what?" Julien felt utter confusion take over his face. Evolet handed his phone to Scarlet, then turned towards Julien.

"The Wolf...is still alive." Evolet chose his words carefully. "I was hoping we'd find this out before anything happened. But apparently we failed."

"Find *what* out?" Julien demanded. "What... Please tell me what's going on." His fingers curved into fists. "I just need to protect Via."

"Keep calm," Evolet warned. He bit his lip. "Okay... No, we *weren't* relying on the police. Not at all. We have had an...er...professional investigator on this since day one."

"Professional investigator?" Julien tilted his head.

"The best aren't usually totally legal," Scarlet spoke up, finally handing her husband's phone back to him. "But we figured we needed the best. And now, apparently, we have Ulven's current address."

Julien leaned back in his chair. "I...see."

"We're only bringing you into this because you're an adult," Evolet went on earnestly, "but you need to understand that it's dangerous."

"I don't care," Julien gritted. "I'm going to help Via."

"Right. We all are," Scarlet nodded. "Okay. So far, we have one lead—Eryka's address. That happens to be in Australia."

"What!" Julien spluttered. "How do you even know she's there?"

"We don't, except for random local camera footage and data from her WiFi and cellular usage," Evolet shrugged. "But we'll find out when we get there."

"You can't actually mean to go there." Julien held his head.

"It's the only real lead we have," Scarlet murmured.

Evolet leaned forward. "Look, nephew—son, I'm asking one thing of you. This will take us four, maybe five days. I know it could be a trap, but either way, something will happen at that address in Australia. Scarlet and I will go there—alone. Can you—and Jaz—hold the fort until we get back, hopefully with Via?"

"I think you're being too optimistic, if we're dealing with the Wolf," Julien sighed, "but I'll do it."

"Thanks." Scarlet stood up. "I'm going to go pack for us, Evy," she called over her shoulder as she headed for the stairs.

Julien slumped miserably. "Uncle Evy...the address isn't even necessarily Eryka's. This could be a ruse to throw you completely off track. I mean, Via was just kidnapped here, and that address is literally halfway across the world."

"I know," Evolet sighed.

"She might have even gone out for a walk," Julien went on. "We still don't know—"

"We found her cell phone in the snow," Evolet reminded him quietly.

"Still—"

"I understand why you don't want to admit that this is happening," Evolet broke in, his face drawn. "I don't want to, either. But I'd rather overreact and find my daughter safe, than wait until it's too late. And I'd like your help for that, Julien Ransom."

Slowly, Julien stood and saluted.

"And you've got it."

* * *

"I'm telling you, it'll look more natural if I go in first, alone," Evolet was arguing, about thirty hours later.

The couple had, at long length, made their way to Australia by plane. The first thing they'd done had been call the family members back at home and get an update. It was quick and not very encouraging. Via had not returned; over twenty-four hours had passed; the police had been duly notified. Moira had urged them to hurry and return home, so they were heading straight for the address, ignoring the fact that it was four in the afternoon local time and felt like two in the morning for them.

"I still think we should go in together," Scarlet muttered. "That'd look even more natural."

"Look, Scar, I'm not going to get hurt," Evolet sighed. "You can—"

"We've arrived," Scarlet interrupted calmly. "Come on. Let's go."

"Scarlet, wait—"

Evolet never finished the sentence; Scarlet grabbed his arm impatiently and pulled him towards the door of the apartment building. The front door opened; it took the two less than sixty seconds to find the designated door. They stood outside it, indecisive.

"How do we know she's even here right now?" Scarlet murmured, after a moment of listening.

"She has a night job," Evolet shrugged. "She *should* be here—she's probably just sleeping. Assuming we're dealing with a normal apartment dweller." He lifted his hand to the door. "I guess we'll find out."

Two loud knocks resounded, echoing through the strangely still apartment building. Almost a minute of silence followed; Scarlet was about to suggest that they give up, when they both heard a muffled shout from inside the room. "Hang on!"

Evolet and Scarlet held their silence. About half a minute later, they both tensed as they heard footsteps that abruptly stopped. They glanced towards the peephole simultaneously, knowing they were being scrutinized.

"What do you want?" came Eryka's voice again. This time it was quieter.

"We need to talk," Evolet answered stiffly. "Open the door or I'll break it down."

"Do you think I'm crazy?" Eryka asked, her voice high in disbelief. "Why are you h—"

Evolet was tired of waiting. Wrapping his hand around the doorknob, he twisted it hard, breaking the lock. Throwing the door open, he marched in, followed by Scarlet, who quickly and quietly shut the door again.

Eryka had gotten dressed quickly, but she was definitely very awake now as she swiftly backed up towards the kitchen counter, slipping her hand into her pocket. "Don't come too close, or I'll call th—"

"You'll do no such thing," Evolet began, but Scarlet moved faster.

"Allow me," she murmured, crossing the distance in an instant and flipping Eryka's hand out of her pocket. She twisted it slightly and held it there. "Young lady, you're going to answer our questions. That's all there is to it—for now, at least. Where is Via?"

But Eryka didn't answer; instead, her face seemed to freeze as she caught her breath. She began to smile sadly, slowly.

Evolet stepped forward, his face hard. "You don't need to act weak."

"I'm not acting, unfortunately," Eryka murmured. "Would you please let go of my arm?"

"Tell us where Via is." Scarlet's eyebrows arched up.

"I don't know," Eryka replied simply. "How should I?"

"Don't play games!" Scarlet's face contorted, and she pushed Eryka away from her, against the kitchen counter. "How are you even still around?"

"I just want to know how you got my address." Eryka bit her lip. "Give me a reason to trust you people. Then maybe I'll tell you what I know."

"*We* give *you* a reason to trust us?" Evolet shook his head in disbelief.

"You've got to be kidding me—" He broke off as Eryka suddenly lifted her right hand and flicked the metal fingers. A set of wolfish claws glinted in the sudden light.

"I no longer have T4," Eryka began slowly, lifting one claw and drawing it across the back of her left hand. A small red line formed, but didn't close as fast as it would have for Scarlet or Evolet. In fact, it didn't even seem to be closing rapidly at all. "I don't know if that changes matters. But I'd like you to know that if you attack me I'm going to do my best to defend myself."

"You don't have T4?" For the first time, Scarlet appeared startled. "But how—"

"I'll tell you the whole story," Eryka interrupted, her eyes narrowing. "I'm just making you aware of the situation."

"We won't hurt you," Evolet sighed. "Tell away."

Eryka headed for the living room, and Evolet and Scarlet followed somewhat cautiously. They followed the twenty-one-year-old's cue and sat down, but were still very much on the alert.

"I woke after six weeks in that coma," Eryka began unceremoniously. "I'm sure you know that it was induced. You probably also know that they took me to the WIPA headquarters for containment."

"It's one of the few superhuman-proof places on this planet," Evolet nodded. "Go on. So you woke up? Six weeks after the incident would've been around when the bomb went off, wouldn't it?" He glanced sideways at Scarlet.

Eryka shrugged. "I don't know why I'm telling you this, because you're not going to believe me. But there was a woman who came in. Asked me if I remembered her. I didn't really, but—"

"What was her name?" Scarlet questioned.

"Lieutenant Diana Anderson," Eryka returned, after a moment's thought. "Why?"

"It sounds familiar," Evolet muttered. "Keep going."

"Well. There's not that much to say," Eryka admitted. "She injected me with something and then let me go. Gave me a passport and plane tickets to Australia. I took my chance to get away, obviously."

"Obviously," Scarlet nodded. "And what then?"

"That's all," Eryka shook her head. "I got a job and eventually an apartment. That's how my life is now. I honestly thought I'd gotten away from it all." She frowned. "Until you two showed up and scared me to death. What did you want to know about Via?"

"She's gone missing," Evolet stated impatiently. "About thirty hours ago. The trail led here."

Eryka's eyebrows shot up. "What trail?"

In answer, Evolet pulled the small plastic bag of papers out of his pocket. "Explain these," he ordered, tossing the bag across the room. He appeared to be somewhat more satisfied when Eryka failed to catch it and had to pick it up from the floor.

"I didn't write these," was Eryka's first comment.

"*Thought* you'd say that," Evolet remarked dryly. "Who did, then?"

"I haven't written like this since I lost my arm," Eryka went on obliviously. She glanced up. "Where'd you get these from?"

"So that's not your handwriting anymore." Scarlet's eyes widened in surprise.

"No, sorry, but it's not," Eryka shook her head. She tossed the bag back, and Evolet caught it easily. "And I wouldn't be threatening Via, either."

"But you—" Scarlet broke off.

"Which reminds me, I never apologized to any of you, did I," Eryka went on. "I remember I was going to do that at some point. Just not yet, because I wasn't supposed to be alive." She bit her lip. "Well, I apologize now. What happens next?"

"I hate situations like this," Evolet muttered. "Well, I guess this was a dead end after all. Scarlet and I should head back to the States, but..." He looked directly at Eryka. "What about you?"

She shrugged. "You're probably going to cart me off to the police station, aren't you? It's not like I can stop you, after all."

"That's what we should do," Scarlet nodded, standing up.

But Eryka stood up as well. "Can I just ask one favor? I know I don't deserve it, but..."

There was something about her eyes that made Evolet feel just a bit sorry for her. He raised his eyebrows. "What is it?"

"I'd like to see Via again before I go," Eryka replied quietly. "They'll kill me, for sure. I just want to talk to Via. If she's okay with that, of course."

"We don't even know where she is." Scarlet shook her head. "We came here hoping to find her."

Eryka smiled slightly. "Then...I'll help you find her."

* * *

"Julien? Julien, where are the kids?"

"Huh?" Julien started awake, to find his aunt Jasmine leaning over him. She sighed, her hands on her hips.

"I thought you were watching the toddlers," the older woman scowled. "And doing homework. Did you drop your laptop on purpose?"

"I...what?" Julien sat up slowly, holding his head. "Ow. Ow. There, it's gone. What? My laptop? I was doing homework..."

He broke off suddenly, staring at his laptop. "I hope I didn't break it. Where are the kids?"

"That's what I want to know," Jasmine muttered. "Well?"

"They were just here a minute ago..."

Julien went silent and listened for a moment. "Wait, where are they?"

"I just got back from the store to find you asleep, with no sign of the kids," Jasmine returned. "This house is way too quiet. How long have you been asleep?"

"I wasn't trying to go to sleep..." Julien muttered. He stood up and picked up his laptop, putting it on the couch. "I don't even remember falling asleep."

His aunt's frown deepened. "Then..."

"No, nothing's happened to them," Julien insisted both to her and to himself. He headed towards the kitchen, but another question from his aunt stopped him in his tracks.

"You do know that you have permanent marker all over your face, don't you?"

"What the blazes?" Julien's eyebrows shot up as he pulled out his phone and stared at his reflection in the dark screen. "Who... That child!"

"Let's keep looking," Jasmine murmured grimly. "If you went to sleep that quickly—" Suddenly she stopped.

"What is it?" Julien paused, turning around to see his aunt standing in the now-open doorway to outside. She'd picked up a paper that had fallen when she opened the door, and was now reading it.

"Great," Jasmine breathed. "They've been taken." She turned to face her nephew. "And the kidnapper has given us an address."

"It's got to be a trap." Julien's face turned nearly white. "Does it say anything about Via?"

Jasmine shook her head, biting her lip. "Nope."

* * *

"This is the worst flight I've ever been on," Scarlet breathed from underneath her light blanket. "Forget about going to sleep."

Evolet, to her right, sighed. "I think I might have to agree with you," he murmured. "It must be storming pretty heavily out there."

"How on earth did *she* do it?" Scarlet wondered softly, glancing sideways at Eryka Ulven. The young woman had fallen asleep against the window and now every worry had smoothed itself out of her face, even as the plane shook and bumped and jolted.

"I don't know," Evolet admitted.

"I don't like this," Scarlet muttered. "This is even worse than landing in a tornado would be."

"You even know what that's like?" Evolet stared at his wife in disbelief.

She shrugged. "I grew up in Kansas, remember? And it was more of a crash landing. And I was seven. And my Mom wouldn't let me go in planes for ten years afterwards."

"Okay." Evolet bit his lip. "Okay. Let's just pray we make it back to the States." He gripped his wife's hand more tightly, glancing at the small screen in front of him. "Though we do have a lot longer to go."

That was when every light in the plane began flashing. Evolet started as multiple people began screaming; the next moment he actually jumped as his oxygen mask fell from the ceiling. He stared at it a moment in shock, then pulled it quickly over his face. However, glancing at Scarlet, Evolet was horrified to see her trying to put Eryka's mask on even before her own.

"Scarlet!" he shouted through the mask. "You're supposed to—"

"I'm fine," Scarlet interrupted as she shoved her own mask on, once Eryka's air supply was safe. The redhead continued shaking Eryka awake. "Come on, the plane is going down!"

"What?" Evolet gaped at her. "No, no, the mask only means that the plane is losing oxygen—"

"We are going to have to land in the water," the speakers throughout the plane began blaring. "Please brace yourselves for impact. Immediately. Please bra—"

The plane shot forward, gradually spiraling down. Each and every passenger slammed forward, screaming, not having had time to brace themselves as ordered. There was one thought in Evolet's mind.

We're not going to make it.

Then, somehow, miraculously, the plane straightened itself somewhat. Everyone caught their breaths, but the plane was still falling, its engines spluttering as the pilot tried to slow the descent. Evolet felt Scarlet let go of his hands, and he opened his eyes, glancing at her.

"Brace yourself," she panted. Evolet managed a weak smile.

"If we're going to go down, let's go down together," he told her, taking her hand again. Holding close for maximum protection, they used their free hands to brace their heads against the backs of the seats in front of them.

The lights kept flashing—faster now. Eryka was somewhat awake now, and she, too, leaned forward and placed her hands and head in impact position. The sound of rushing air became louder and louder…something was beeping in the background. Everyone in the plane was silent, except for some young girl who was crying somewhere closer to the front of the plane.

Then they hit the water.

It was a horribly rough landing, one that kept on jolting as the plane seemed to skid across the surface of the water. Evolet clenched his teeth, biting back the shout that threatened to break free. Other people screamed. But finally, mercifully, it stopped.

Evolet unbuckled himself preemptively and stood up, feeling the plane rock gently in what was most definitely water. The strange thing was that his feet felt...wet.

He glanced down at his shoes and saw it, just as Scarlet realized the same thing. The floor of the plane had already flooded.

"We are going to have to evacuate the plane," some flight attendant shouted from the front of the plane. "Can we please have those in exit rows wait for the order to open their exits... Please, no one leave your seat. Please do not panic. The situation is under control. I repeat, please do *not* panic."

"Where are we?" someone yelled.

"We are near an island," came the answer. "It won't be too hard for the rafts to make it safely ashore. Please do not panic. Again, the situation is under control."

"An island?" Evolet raised his eyebrows. "There's got to be a reason she's not giving us details."

"It's Reunion Island," Eryka spoke up, and both adults glanced at her in surprise. Eryka gestured towards her display. "And the water there...is full of sharks."

"Keep that quiet," Scarlet hissed. "If people hear that, everything is over!"

She glanced towards Evolet. "What do we do next?"

* * *

Two minutes later found Evolet and Scarlet busily engaged in helping people into one of the rafts. The first one was almost full, when it was Eryka's turn in line.

"I'll wait," she decided abruptly, gesturing to the person behind her to go ahead.

"No, you don't," Scarlet shook her head. "We'll see you on land. There you go."

Minutes passed, and the plane sunk deeper in the water. The first raft was cast off, then the second, then the third. Only a few people remained to get into the fourth, including the plane personnel and Evolet and Scarlet, but the young couple practically forced the personnel to go first.

"We'll be right along," they insisted.

"You can't stay, it's dangerous—" the pilot began.

Scarlet fairly shoved him into the raft, and Evolet cut the rope.

"Go on!" he shouted out the door, into the pouring rain and cracking thunder outside.

Then the two were alone. Dripping wet, Scarlet and Evolet turned to each other and grinned simultaneously.

"Ready to battle some sharks?" Evolet asked, and Scarlet nodded, taking a deep breath as the two of them grabbed hold of the door to the cockpit and jerked it off its hinges.

The impact knocked them into the seats, but they were up almost immediately, and back in the cockpit. Evolet wrenched a piece of metal controls off the control board, handed it to Scarlet, and then scavenged a weapon for himself. The plane was even lower in the water now; there were mere minutes left before it would sink.

Without wasting another moment, the two shoved the door out into the sea and jumped out after it, jerking the tabs to inflate their life vests in the same moment. Scarlet grabbed the door first, and then glanced at Evolet, who nodded furiously.

"Get on!" he shouted. "I'll take the first turn!"

Nodding, Scarlet scrambled aboard the door and clung to it as her husband grabbed hold of the edge and began swimming with all his might, in the direction the rafts had taken. But Scarlet watched ahead, and now her blue eyes widened in horror.

"Evolet...the rafts!"

"Oh no," Evolet breathed, even as his wife leapt recklessly into the water and struck out like an Olympic champion for the rafts, weapon in hand. Taking a deep breath, he plunged into the water after her, leaving the door behind.

* * *

Thirty minutes followed. Over thirty minutes. Filled with blood, screaming, water, and sharks.

Only one raft made it to shore. There had been four rafts, all full of people, but Scarlet and Evolet had only managed to save one. The others had been torn to shreds. Bits and pieces floated on the surface of the night storm water, mingling with blood—both human and shark.

Evolet and Scarlet collapsed on the sand, panting and utterly exhausted. They had had so many narrow escapes. They, too, had lost blood. But even yet, their job wasn't finished.

Leaving those in the safely-grounded raft to recover, the two superhuman adults headed back down the shore, hoping to hear or see survivors. Evolet scanned the nearly pitch black horizon, sighing as he realized no one else could have possibly survived.

It was Scarlet who shouted to him before abruptly leaping into the water and swimming desperately for some dark shape that Evolet now recognized to be a person.

In reality, it was two people.

Together, Scarlet and Evolet dragged the two ashore. Evolet started when he saw that the older girl, whose arms were wrapped around a girl of about six or seven, was Eryka. Her face and clothes were saturated with blood, almost more so than with water. Her wolf claws were extended. She had a jagged cut across her face, and her chest was bleeding heavily. In comparison, the unknown little girl was unhurt, suffering only from a few scratches.

Gently, Scarlet separated the little girl from Eryka's protective embrace, lying her down on the beach and checking her pulse. She was alive.

"I don't know about Ulven," Scarlet heard her husband mutter.

Turning, Scarlet shook her head as she knelt down next to Eryka.

"She's unconscious, and she's losing blood fast," Scarlet diagnosed. "We could save her if we got her to a hospital...now." Yet even as she spoke, her hands were busy as she tried to stop the young woman's bleeding.

"Concussion for both of them, too, probably," Evolet murmured. "Can I help?"

Scarlet bit her lip. "Not unless you can find a hospital."

Her husband glanced up, at the heavily storming sky. Then around, at the wild-looking beach area deserted by all but the crash survivors. "So there's no way to save her?"

Scarlet sighed, glancing up at him. "I can think of only one way. It'll speed up her healing and probably save her life. But that way is…"

"T4," Evolet finished, sighing in turn. "Do we trust her? We could be saving a life…or resurrecting a monster."

Scarlet smoothed away the bloodstained hair from the young woman's bleeding face and glanced at it a moment, silently.

Eryka's eyes were closed. Her breathing was heavy and ragged as she struggled for breath. But for that, her face was peaceful. Like that of a child asleep… Trusting. And yet, suffering.

And in that moment, Scarlet knew that, despite how many people Eryka had murdered, despite the amount of damage she'd done in the world—even despite what she'd done to Scarlet's own daughter—there was no way Scarlet could sit by and let Eryka die, without giving her one last chance.

"She saved the girl," Scarlet reasoned aloud, her face decisive as she leaned back. "She risked her own life to save this child."

"How are you going to do it?" Evolet questioned warily. "Or do you want m—" He broke off, shaking his head in some mixture of shock and admiration. "I must say, that looked violent."

"It was," Scarlet returned shortly, finishing the somewhat deep cut she'd made in her own arm, then pulling aside the makeshift bandaging to let her own blood mingle with Eryka's. "Let's hope this works, because if it doesn't, I don't think there's any way to fix this."

"Scar," Evolet interrupted after a few moments. "I think that's enough. We don't need you badly hurt, too."

"I'm fine," Scarlet insisted. "But I think that's enough, too." Slowly, she wrapped the remnants of her jacket around her arm. "It had *better* work," she gritted. "But she's cut pretty deeply, so it should get right to work."

"Are you sure you're fine?" Evolet raised his eyebrows.

"Yes," Scarlet answered shortly. "How is the girl?"

They both bent over the younger girl, who was beginning to stir uneasily. Scarlet picked her up carefully, holding her in her lap and smoothing her short blond-tinged brown hair.

"It's alright," she murmured to the girl, who was coming awake. "You're safe now."

"Mommy," was the first thing the girl whispered, before her eyes opened. Suddenly Evolet choked.

"It's okay," Scarlet went on as a slight smile came over her face. "You're okay. Are you awake now?"

The girl's eyes opened, and she stared at Scarlet. Her eyes were a bright blue.

"Where's Mommy?" she asked in Mexican-accented English, leaning back in Scarlet's arms to inspect her more thoroughly.

"I don't know," Scarlet admitted. She began to stand up. "Let's—"

"No!" The girl had seen Eryka lying on the sand, and now she wriggled herself free from the startled Scarlet, falling to her knees almost right away from weakness. "I want—to stay—with her."

Scarlet and Evolet exchanged glances, and Evolet nodded. "I'll go see if anyone knows anything," he offered, heading up the beach towards the group from the raft.

The girl stared up at Scarlet again. This time, the blue eyes were filled with worry. "Is she...is she okay?"

"I hope so." Scarlet bent down at Eryka's side again, feeling her wrist for a pulse. "At least she's still hanging on." Scarlet nodded to herself. "I think...I think she's getting stronger. She might even wake up soon." The redheaded adult smiled at the much younger girl.

The girl smiled back. "I hope so. She's my friend. She saved me."

"What's your name?" Scarlet wondered aloud.

"Gwen," the girl answered. "Gwendolyn Genevieve Cruz."

"That's a nice name," Scarlet smiled. "Mine's Scarlet."

Gwendolyn raised her small eyebrows. "I can call you that?"

"You can call me Mrs. Whyte," Scarlet amended. "Is that better?"

The girl nodded, then glanced towards Eryka. "What's her name?"

"Let's see if she wakes up and is ready to tell you," Scarlet decided, sitting down next to the little girl.

It was strange how much this night reminded her of that one over two years ago, on the New York shore by the bridge. Scarlet was half a world away, but she was still filled with the same peace, the same calm-after-the-storm.

She couldn't help but smile at seeing Gwendolyn sat so close to Eryka's right shoulder, so close to the metal arm which had been the terror of New York but which had probably also saved this girl from certain death. Yes, now Scarlet was sure she had made the right choice. Eryka would be changed... Or so Scarlet hoped.

She glanced up the beach, where her husband was apparently helping some other men to use the raft to build a shelter. Despite the tragedy, they'd survived. Now the Whytes, as well as the other survivors, would have to find their own ways home, just as soon as they contacted local authorities for help. Somehow, the situation seemed so far away from Scarlet's troubles at home. She sighed, frowning, as she remembered... Via was missing, and Scarlet and Evolet had perhaps never been further from finding her.

Time passed. Scarlet did her best to keep both Gwendolyn and Eryka warm, until Evolet and some other men came with a makeshift stretcher for Eryka. Evolet insisted upon carrying Gwendolyn to the tent as well; he was very obviously worried for Scarlet's strength. But they all found shelter, and gradually some sort of warmth. But no one had seen Gwendolyn's mother. Evolet and Scarlet chose not to tell her, not yet. Though, from the expression on the girl's face that lingered through the night, she had already guessed.

The dawn broke. It was a lovely, unsurpassed pink that tinged the horizon, much to everyone's delight. Cheers rang through the air; with the day, would surely come the end of the storm, and the end of the waiting. Help would be found. Perhaps help was already on the way.

As the cheering finished, Eryka opened her eyes. Gwendolyn was the first to notice.

"Thank you," she murmured, slipping her hand into the older young woman's. Eryka smiled weakly, sitting up.

"How do you feel?" Scarlet asked anxiously, and Evolet came close to hear the answer.

It was quiet, yet confident. "Suspiciously well."

* * *

What with Evolet's talent for avoiding newsmen and police, and Scarlet's anxiety to return home, the Whytes found themselves back in the States soon enough. Somehow they cleared most of the legal hurdles, promising to return to the case later. For now, they had an emergency at home to attend to.

Eryka came with them—and so did Gwendolyn, for the time being, at least. It had turned out that Gwendolyn had lost her only remaining parent in the crash; her father had passed away years before. And Gwendolyn had clung to and insisted upon staying with Eryka. Nothing could change her mind—to the point that she had managed to sneak and follow them. She would have to go back, the Whytes knew—they just didn't have time, not now. And it had been complicated enough smuggling Eryka in.

Much to Scarlet's and Evolet's relief, though Eryka was once again super-human, she showed no signs of making any trouble. She was the image of helpfulness, even offering to drive the family home from their final stop at the New York airport. Though Evolet rejected the offer, he was now practically certain of the young woman's truthfulness.

So they drove home together, Gwendolyn asleep in the backseat with Eryka. The little girl's head was cushioned by her rescuer's arms, as if Eryka was still shielding her from anything that could possibly hurt her. It was a picture that made Scarlet smile sadly. The two could have been born to be sisters...but with Eryka's criminal record, that future wasn't even a possibility.

They hadn't been able to contact either Jasmine or Julien. Both the adults' phones had been lost in the crash, as well as everything else they'd had with them, which thankfully hadn't been much. They had tried to contact their relatives upon their arrival in the United States, but that had failed. Supposedly, however, the police would be contacting Moira Whyte, who would try to get through to Jasmine. Moira and Conner were living only a few blocks

115

away from the younger Whyte generation's house, so Evolet and Scarlet hoped that things would all be well.

And so Evolet drove through the night. It snowed lightly, and gradually Eryka fell asleep as well.

But when they finally arrived, it disturbed Evolet that all the lights were off. Of course, it was one in the morning, but he would've expected either Jasmine or Julien to be waiting for them.

Turning off the car, Evolet motioned to Scarlet to wait in the vehicle, and then hurried up the steps to the house. He tested the door, just in case, before knocking.

It wasn't locked. Evolet pulled the door open to face a pitch-black, terrifyingly empty kitchen.

Slowly, cautiously, he turned on the light. There was nothing there.

He walked through the entire house, finding nothing anywhere he went. It reminded him of something from a horror movie. Every turn he took, he was expecting something, someone to jump out at him...almost even hoping. But nothing happened.

All the beds were empty, even the toddlers'. No one was in the living room. No one was in the kitchen. No one was even in the storm shelter. To put it shortly...the house had been evacuated.

Evolet made his way back out to the car, unable to shake the feeling of terror off him. It only got worse when he saw Scarlet through the car window—asleep.

Panicking, Evolet ran around the vehicle and jerked his door open, tapping Scarlet's shoulder and calling for her to wake up. She didn't twitch a muscle.

It was then that Evolet noticed the overwhelming smell of nothingness that had pervaded the car. As the realization hit him, he fell out of the car, already losing control of his senses. He pulled his new phone out of his pocket as he knelt there in the newly-fallen snow and tried to call 9-1-1... His hands shook strangely as he punched the numbers in with agonizing slowness.

Then the device was kicked away from him. Startled, Evolet glanced up, only to see the same sort of thing he had been expecting to see in the house.

She was tall, her body completely covered in some kind of dark, armored suit. There was both a knife and a gun clipped onto her belt, but the weapon she was carrying at the moment was a small syringe.

Her head and face were almost completely covered with a hard-material helmet and mask, leaving only her eyes visible. They were young and were what told Evolet that his attacker was a woman—a very young one.

He had just enough time to realize that, somehow, the bluish, purplish eyes that met his own were strangely blank...

Then his attacker leaned down in a swift, sleek movement, and the tip of the syringe she carried found its way into Evolet's wrist.

Evolet didn't even feel the sting. He just felt the brief moment of his falling backwards as everything went completely and horribly black.

* * *

Eryka was awake, but she hadn't yet chosen to open her eyes. There was nothing but silence around her, silence that reminded her strangely of her six coma weeks.

She was lying down, her hands and feet restrained behind her back; she guessed she was on the floor, because of how cold the surface was, but it was still too much like her coma for her to dare to try to open her eyes. Because the realization that she couldn't would be worse than the uncertainty.

Yet finally she gave in, and was relieved to find that she had not been deprived of the sense of vision. However, if she was completely honest with herself, the situation wasn't much better.

She was indeed on the floor, as was everyone else, though most of them were still asleep. Twisting her head around, Eryka caught sight of Julien, Conner, Jasmine, Evolet, Scarlet, Gwen—everyone except for Via. Involuntarily, Eryka sighed as she struggled to sit up.

Finally she managed it, and she pushed herself up against the wall, trying for a few moments to break whatever held her hands together. She failed, but that fact didn't much surprise her.

Glancing around, Eryka realized where they were. They were in a large containment room at what had been the New York WIPA Center.

The floor and walls were charred with remains from the fire two years ago, and the whole atmosphere was that of a deserted building, which made Eryka realize they were on their own in the middle of the countryside, in a wrecked building that no one bothered to visit. The thought chilled her as she sat and watched the others come awake.

First was the two-year-old Whyte boy. Eryka didn't know him, but she'd heard Evolet and Scarlet discussing their two young children briefly. Suddenly Eryka found herself looking for the one-year-old girl…but, like Via, Lily Whyte was missing.

"Where are we?" Evolet Whyte asked Eryka softly, and she glanced at him, not a muscle of her face twitching. She'd known he was watching her.

"Where I was taken during my coma," she answered quietly. "This place was built to withstand superhumans."

Groaning, Evolet pulled himself up as well. "Well, everyone's here but Lily and Via. And Aunt Moira. I wonder how long it's going to take everyone to wake up." He winced as he tried to break the bonds that held his hands behind his back.

Eryka raised her eyebrows slightly. "Don't bother," she told him. "It's not going to work."

"No choice but to try," Evolet mumbled, but he gave in anyway, almost grudgingly. "What's next?"

About half an hour passed before everyone was awake. The last to awaken was Gwendolyn, but by the time her eyes opened, things were already in motion. The door to the room had been opened, and two new people had come in.

One of them was the same masked, silent bodyguard-slash-hitman that had taken Evolet out. Incidentally, Julien remembered her as well. But most of the Whytes' attention was focused on the hitman's companion. Someone who seemed vaguely familiar, and who was carrying a strongly sleeping Lily Whyte. And holding a gun to the one-year-old's chest.

"Glad to see you're all awake," she addressed them in a thick British accent. "I'm sure we're all glad to meet again. Especially *you*, Eryka."

And yet, still, Eryka's face didn't change. "It's her," she announced in a voice everyone could hear. "Lieutenant Diana Anderson."

Julien didn't remember the name, but he couldn't help but notice the way his aunt Jasmine stiffened. He glanced behind him, back at Eryka, who nodded slightly.

"Put my daughter down," Evolet spoke up, his face and voice both angry, though his voice spoke of hidden levels of fury. "I don't care what you think our position is. If you hurt her, the game is over."

"But there is no game," Diana laughed, glancing towards her seemingly mute sidekick. "Or is there, Shadow?"

The specter shook her head once.

"Look, Whytes, I want only one thing from you before I kill you all with poison gas," Diana went on, her tones suddenly getting serious. "Who is your investigator?"

Scarlet and Evolet exchanged glances, while everyone stared at them in surprise, except Julien and Eryka. "How would we know?" Evolet asked finally.

No one noticed Julien and Eryka nod stiffly to each other. "You *have* to know," Diana frowned. "Look, let's have an example. What time is it, Ms. Wolf? Or do you not—"

"I do," Eryka interrupted calmly, her gray eyes hard as steel. "The time...is your midnight."

She nodded to Julien, kicking out at him with a giant burst of superhuman energy that launched him across the room. Landing on his feet directly in front of Diana, Julien snatched Lily Whyte away from the former WIPA Lieutenant, taking the bullet she fired in his back. Julien fell forward for a moment before he caught himself, diving towards Scarlet and fairly tossing her the one-year-old. One by one the superhumans stood up, all but Eryka. Julien rubbed his back ruefully where his purple jacket had stopped the bullet.

"How... How are you..." Diana spluttered in horror and hatred, taking a step backwards. "How are your hands free?"

"They're not, actually, but that doesn't make me entirely useless," Eryka spoke up, standing up despite the fact that her hands were still tied behind her back. Her claws were out. "And I'm not going to let you kill this family because of me."

Screaming in rage, Diana lifted her gun once more and began shooting at Eryka, but once again it was Julien who got in the way. Moving like lightning, he knocked the gun away and shoved the Lieutenant up face-forward against the wall. "Where do you have Via?" he hissed.

"Shadow, don't let them get away!" Diana shouted.

Muttering something under his breath, Julien pulled a needle out of Diana's own belt and stuck her in the wrist with it. Diana collapsed to the floor, and Julien wheeled around, only to see the masked hitman in the very act of pouncing at him.

The fight that followed was one-sided. Julien found himself losing in almost every way to this strangely silent, yet determined superhuman who seemed intent on destroying him. But it lasted only a minute or so before Julien felt the weight on his back disappear. He scrambled to his feet to see Eryka locked in a hold with the "Shadow."

"They're going," Eryka told him needlessly.

But what followed next was definitely not what Julien had been expecting from the former "Wolf."

"Take Gwendolyn...and get her out of here."

"What?" he shouted back, more confused than he'd ever been in his life.

"There's a gas system and we don't know when it will go off!" Eryka screamed at him. "Take Gwen and go! I will keep this maniac off our backs!"

She was already hard-pressed, Julien realized. He glanced around and saw the seven-year-old Gwendolyn running towards him. Wrapping his strong arms around her, he turned and followed the others.

Eryka was the last one in the room.

"Don't stay there forever," Julien called after him. "You escape, too..."

Eryka never answered. Her opponent was stronger than her and was pushing her slowly but steadily towards the doorway.

The "Wolf" fought back with all her might, filled with a desperate will to hold the silent soldier back as long as she could before she had to yield the way. Eryka didn't hesitate to use her claws, but they achieved practically nothing—until some minutes later, by which time Eryka felt her strength fading quickly. But she managed to catch her claws at the base of the mask, and she jerked it away, vehemently, her claws digging deep into the soldier's face as she did so.

Eryka's mind went blank as the mask fell in two pieces and blood streamed from the left side of her opponent's face. It was so much déjà-vu, all at once, that Eryka didn't even see the next blow coming. Her opponent followed her to the ground, holding her down, and yet Eryka could only stare.

"Via?" she gasped out in shock.

There was no answer, at least not verbally. Instead, Via Whyte reached for the knife at her belt, pulling it free in a swift, fluid movement. She lifted it, ready to strike.

"Via," Eryka panted, staring in horror at her former friend's eyes. They were unusually cloudy, not to mention completely without expression. Almost without consciousness.

Eryka's metal hand flew out in pure instinct as the knife came flying down at her.

She caught the first strike, but not the second, nor the third. Desperately, bruised and battered and now bleeding in two potentially vital places, Eryka could think of only one thing to be done. Using her claws, she slashed the knife away from Via, cutting the girl's knuckles in the process. Then, in one last desperate move, she jerked Via close, twisting the girl's hands and arms together.

Still under the influence of whatever Diana had drugged her with, Via relentlessly began to tug herself free. But there was still blood running down her face, and now, finally, Via's actions became slow and weak. Finally she stopped struggling.

Eryka's hands fell away out of pure exhaustion, and she fell back, gasping for breath in convulsions that nearly doubled her up. She could taste blood in her mouth, and there was a horrible sensation that she was drowning.

A foot or two away from her, she was vaguely aware that Via was sitting against the wall and staring ahead of her with dead eyes. Maybe Via was coming out of it, Eryka realized, but nobody or nothing could save Eryka now.

I get to die the hero after all.

But still it seemed incomplete, unfinished, even after Eryka's eyes shut for the last time. There was a strange silence, except for Eryka's and Via's raspy breathing—but the silence was suddenly broken by a loud, piercing scream that echoed between the solid walls and made even Eryka flinch.

"No!"

Finally. It was Via's voice.

"Please...let this be a nightmare..."

"Via," Eryka managed somehow, despite the coughing that had suddenly overtaken her. "I'm...sorry."

"How are you here?" Via questioned, her entire world fallen to pieces as she knelt there, crying, by the side of her coughing, dying once-upon-a-time friend. "Where did everyone go? Why...why am I here?"

She stopped her questions as the truth hit her for the first time. "No...this... was me... Eryka! I don't...I don't hate you!"

Her tears slid down her cheek, mingling with the blood that was still coming.

"Don't die, not now!"

Eryka's mouth opened as she coughed again, but this time words came out as well. "Then...are we still...best friends..."

"Forever!" Via sobbed. "No...what is happening..."

She wrapped her hand tightly around Eryka's, and Eryka squeezed back. For one brief moment.

Then it was over as Eryka coughed blood, one last time.

"This is a nightmare..." Panicking and confused, Via felt desperately for Eryka's pulse. There was none, and Via stood up, glancing around her for the first time.

Her head was free from the helmet-mask now, but she still didn't look like herself. Her long hair had been cut short, and her face was drenched with blood, as were the strange combat clothes she wore.

She didn't know where she was. She didn't know *when* she was.

There was only one thought in her head:

This was not real life.

She was dreaming.

But her face hurt. Her entire body hurt. But worst of all, her mind hurt.

This was no dream—no nightmare.

This was...reality.

Via fell forward, screaming again. "Eryka!"

But the awakening had come too late.

Book Six: Trooper Z

Frankfurt, Germany.
Summer 2068.
WIPA Scientific Base.

He knew, as soon as he opened his eyes, that something was different.

He had slept long—too long. He should have been awakened by now, by the automatic light if not by the call to breakfast. And yet the room light had not turned on. Neither had the hallway light.

Suddenly the boy sat up, staring as he realized that the door was open.

* * *

The dark hallway was as quiet as if no one had walked through it in a thousand years, but that changed as the tall, silent, white-clothed boy stepped through it softly. He was dressed from head to toe in white, semi-hazmat-style clothing, from high-collared jacket to tall boots that overlapped with his somewhat baggy pants. On his neck was tattooed the identification *Z-021DON*.

His face and eyes were young, but he seemed tall for his age. His closely-cut hair was of a dark brown color, and his eyes were green.

Stepping into the large room at the end of the hallway, he saw that it was completely empty. The boy's eyes widened. The large, long table he and his companions usually breakfasted at was still there, but there was not a soul within the room. Not a single sound except for the ones he made.

The boy went back down the hall, stopping at each doorway and whispering a name loudly. No one answered him. At the last door, the one opposite his own, the boy paused hesitantly, and then bit his lip before knocking anyway.

"Gän?" he asked, with the same facial expression as if he might be disturbing a mad dog.

But there was not the slightest sign that he wasn't the only person alive within a radius of five miles.

The boy tried the big doors at the end of the hallway. It was obvious that he hadn't expected them to open—but they did. Gingerly, as if he was scared he'd be caught by seemingly nonexistent authorities, the boy tiptoed into the next room.

He walked down that hallway, and down another, and down another. It didn't take him long to get lost. But finally he opened a door marked *Ausgang*, and suddenly the boy found himself standing on the edge of a back street.

He blinked in the sudden sunlight, stepping forward mechanically and then jumping back as a car shot past. Startled, the boy let go of the door; it slammed shut behind him.

Dazed as he was, it wasn't hard for the boy to realize that he didn't belong out here. Suddenly panicking, he tried to pull the door open again, but it had locked automatically.

The boy's eyes widened in surprise and horror. He tried again, wrapping his hand tightly around the steel knob; but all he succeeded in was pulling the knob off the door. But the door was even heavier than the knob, and simply would not budge.

Scowling, the boy kicked the door hard before walking off and ignoring the fact that it did jar somewhat.

He stopped at the corner of the building, shaking his head to try to clear the dizzy feeling. He was half-unaware of his surroundings, perhaps because he had never been in a place like this before.

The streets were strange to him. So was the open sky. So were the tall buildings.

The crowd felt menacing. There were so many people, all of them dressed differently. For a boy who'd only ever known uniform clothing for himself and his companions, the variety of the crowd's dressing habits was simply—but shockingly—unheard of.

The boy was alone, unwanted, unknown—a stranger. He could feel it, in the way that the few people who did notice him, stared for a few moments before moving on. The boy wondered if, perhaps, he should move on as well. But where could he go?

The sun beat down on his face as he followed the tall, concrete-walled building he'd come out of, all the way to the main entrance. But the entrance was boarded over, spray-painted. It seemed as if an angry mob had attacked the place.

Above the door were the words, *WIPA Sc. B. 02*

The boy stared up at the lettering, his face devoid of any emotion except that of quiet fear. He knew *those* letters, at least. *WIPA.* They were somewhere on everything the boy had ever made use of in his life. All over the building. Even on the tags of the clothes he wore—and in small letters on his neck, below the ID.

The boy's hands went up to his neck automatically as the thought struck him, and he unfolded his collar so that it went up nearly to his chin, covering all the letters. This building was WIPA. So was he, that was for sure. And if the popular feeling seemed to be against WIPA...

At least the boy was tolerably certain that he could get back inside through this entrance, if he had to. But right now he was free...whatever *that* meant. He could very well be in massive trouble. And what was he supposed to do in a world like this one?

Suddenly he felt a hand touch his shoulder. The boy spun around instinctively, grabbing the person's wrist and pinning him against the wall in about half a second.

The other boy swallowed hard, staring terrifiedly at the white-clad boy, who slowly let go, stepping back. It was clear that, though the older, white-dressed boy was definitely much stronger, both were equally afraid of each other.

"Hey, are you lost?" the younger, civilian-clad boy spoke up finally, in German.

The stronger boy continued staring, almost as if he didn't comprehend the question. The younger boy plucked up his courage.

"Say, you aren't fresh out from prison, are you?" He stepped closer, glancing hard at the boy's white clothes. "No, those aren't prison clothes. I should know. My older brother's been in and out six times."

He finished the sentence proudly, as if it was an accomplishment, but the announcement still elicited no reaction from the silent older boy.

"Hey, you aren't from an asylum, are you?" the younger boy asked suddenly, taking a step back again as his eyes widened. If this kid was from an asylum, he could definitely be dangerous.

"I don't..." The older boy shook his head, obviously wondering whether or not to trust his new acquaintance. "I don't know."

"Me, neither," the twelve-year-old agreed affably. "You look American. So American I bet you could speak English. What are you doing here?"

"I don't know," the white-clad boy said again. He took a deep breath before gesturing towards the WIPA building. "I'm...I'm from there."

"You're from there?" The boy stared in shock. "There's only adults in there. Or there were. They all left last night. I saw them."

"No, there weren't only adults." The older boy struggled for the German words. "There were twelve of us...of boys like me. I was left behind."

"Why were you in there?" the younger boy asked curiously. "It's a science place, isn't it?"

The older boy bit his lip. "I don't know... I guess so. I've *always* been there."

The younger boy nodded to himself. "Well, I guess you're on your own now. You can come with me; I'll find you something to eat. What's your name?"

The other boy's hand crept up to his neck, where his collar hid the numbers and letters. "My name...is Don."

"Don what?" The younger boy took Don's hand, pulling him down the street. "My name's Franz. Franz Schäfen."

Don let himself be pulled along. "That's all," he murmured. "It's just Don."

* * *

Franz was a very extroverted German twelve-year-old, and it didn't take him long to knit the first strands of a strange sort of friendship between himself and the abnormal boy who called himself Don. The friendship was further fostered by the fact that Franz was somewhat eager to offer his new friend some of Franz's older brother's hand-me-downs. Don seemed to come alive a bit—even more so when Franz found him some breakfast.

"Is it good?" the younger boy asked anxiously, sitting down for a moment before jumping up again to pace around the kitchen. "It's my brother's. He's going to kill me when he gets me back."

"I won't let him kill you," Don offered, shoveling the food away ravenously. It was past noon by now, and Don hadn't had breakfast—though he felt as if he hadn't eaten in a week. "Are you hungry?"

"No, I'm fine," Franz insisted, shaking his head.

Don glanced him over thoroughly for the first time. He saw a thin, yet cheery golden-haired boy with a strong jaw and scrawny muscles. Yet the boy seemed beaten-up and bruised. Franz was dressed in worn-out clothes like the ones he'd given Don to put over Don's white outfit. The room they were in appeared to be what had once been the living room of a small apartment, but Don didn't know any such terms. He didn't yet have a word for the dirt that colored the floor, or for the paper that peeled from the walls, or the broken glass that decorated the window frame, but Don did realize that the room wasn't in ideal condition.

"You live here?" Don asked, and the younger boy nodded energetically.

"My brother and I. I was born here. But Mom's long gone and Dad's been in prison for just about my entire life." It was clear from Franz's face that he didn't care much—or at least pretended not to. "How about you?"

Don shrugged. "I don't remember anything except that...building."

"Then how do you even know what a mom or a dad is?" Franz questioned curiously.

The older boy's face was emotionless. "There were other boys there. Some had had families. Most didn't remember, though, just like I don't remember."

"Say, where'd all those other boys go?" Franz wondered.

"No idea," Don replied unhelpfully. He stood up abruptly, then stared at his plastic bowl. "Um—"

"Just toss it in the sink," Franz shrugged. "My brother will make me wash it tonight, when he gets back."

"Thought you said he'd kill you," Don muttered to himself, following orders anyway. He glanced back at the German boy. "Alright, what's next?"

"What's next?" The twelve-year-old grinned impishly. "First you tell me your life story. Then I'll tell you mine."

"There's nothing to tell." Don frowned, touching his high collar once again. "Really, there's...nothing to tell."

"Well, what were you and those other boys locked up in there for?" the German questioned obstinately. "Wait, is it a reformatory?"

"I don't *think* so." Don bit his lip. "It was just a building. A school, a training ground..." He caught his breath suddenly as a vague memory came to him. "A laboratory. That's all it was. Now tell me about you."

"Fine," Franz sighed, abruptly sitting down on the floor, against the wall. "I already told you my parents are gone. I've got one older brother—his name is Wolfgang—and I had a younger sister. At least, that's what Wolfie says." The boy twisted his lip. "My brother and I live here now. He's out all day and most of the night...he has a job," Franz explained evasively, with the first hint of secrecy that Don had seen from him yet. "I don't really, not yet. Uhh...I do some stuff though. In the group."

"What kind of stuff?" Don asked. It was an innocent enough question, to Don, but apparently the answer wasn't that simple to Franz.

"Um...just stuff." The German boy yawned loudly. "What do you plan to do, Don?"

"I don't know," Don admitted reflectively. "I have absolutely no experience with this kind of world before. Any suggestions?"

Franz half-smiled. "Maybe."

* * *

And that was how Don found himself invited to become a part of the gang.

When Franz's older brother Wolfgang returned home late that night, he was in a bad mood, to say the least. He marched straight into the bedroom and picked up the form on the bed by the back of the collar. Naturally, the suddenly-awakened Don defended himself, ending by slamming the startled twenty-three-year-old Wolfgang against the wall and demanding sleepily who in blazes *he* was supposed to be.

Franz came belatedly to his older brother's rescue, explaining the situation and pleading, somewhat reluctantly and at Wolfgang's urgent request—more like command—for Don to let the young man go. Don did so, stepping away, but then Wolfgang flew at him, muttering something in German that Don was personally glad he didn't understand.

Catching Wolfgang by the wrist, Don made a neat twist, leaving Wolfgang to discover himself on the floor a moment later with an exquisitely, painfully twisted hand.

"Uh, Don?" Franz's voice was somewhat cautious.

"Yes?" Don replied, without even glancing at the younger boy behind him. He kept his narrowed eyes on Wolfgang as the much older man glared at him.

"Please don't hurt him," Franz whispered, still sounding as if he was in awe. "He's, uh, my brother, remember?"

"Oh, yeah." Don nodded briskly, offering a hand to help Wolfgang up. "Sorry about that."

The young man rejected the hand, muttering unclassified German words once again as he pulled himself up, breathing heavily. "Where'd you pick up this mad dog?" he asked Franz angrily. Neither Schäfen boy noticed that Don winced at the expression.

"He's escaped from the WIPA base," Franz explained eagerly. "And he's got nothing to do and nowhere to go. Won't he make a great addition to the crowd?"

"Over my dead body," Wolfgang hissed. "I'm going to kill him. I'm going to wring his little neck."

"Not yet, please." Franz's tones were meek and submissive. "I'll wash the dishes now if you don't."

"You little—!" Wolfgang reached for his younger brother, only to find Don suddenly in his path.

"Don't touch him," the fourteen-year-old warned quietly. "Franz is my friend. If you touch him, I'll show you exactly why you won't and *can't* kill me."

Wolfgang stared at him with a mix of horror and fury. "Who are you, you little weasel?"

The boy shrugged. "The name's Don."

* * *

Despite Wolfgang's enmity, Don found his way into the group soon enough. He was good at anything that required strength—and even better at anything that required fighting.

Except, Don wouldn't fight.

The already-tense situation accelerated one night, and quite suddenly, too. The gang leader, a hot-headed German-Dane named Gerold Lund, was a bit off in the head that night and wanted to know why in blazes "Don" couldn't go and beat up their enemy gang. Maybe even take out their leader.

"Are you scared?" he taunted. "I bet you're perfectly capable. Right, boys?"

Don met the much older man's eyes. "I'm not scared," he replied calmly, frowning.

"What, then?" someone called out. Bernardo Krause. He just happened to have run into the other gang earlier that day, and had made it away with a black eye and a broken nose. "What are you waiting for? They need payback!"

"If you want to pay them back, do it yourself," Don shrugged. "They haven't hurt me. I'm not interested."

"This isn't about you. It's about our group," the leader hissed angrily, tossing an empty glass bottle against the concrete wall of the abandoned port shipping building. It shattered noisily. "You're one of us now. Act like it!"

"Sorry, but I already said that I don't care to go attack them." Don's green eyes narrowed into slits.

The man fairly spluttered in rage. "We're feeding you, kid! We're clothing you, protecting you..." He shook his head in disgust. "Why won't you help us?"

"I don't want to go hurting people unless they give me a reason to," Don sighed, while about half the group around him and the leader booed. "Why should I? As far as I can see, this is a bit of a useless war between you and them, and I don't think it needs to be that way. I don't care to get involved, thank you."

"You *what?*" The leader's mouth dropped open in shock. "You're...a traitor! If you aren't for us, then you're against us!"

He lunged forward, grabbing another glass bottle off the table next to him. The next moment was chaos. Don defended himself, and the leader ended up sprawling half-dazed on the hard concrete ground. Then the other members of the gang attacked Don as well. Though a few seemed to be on his side. Including Franz.

"Leave him alone! He doesn't have to do it," the boy shouted, his high-pitched voice ringing above the others'.

Then he screamed as one of the gang member's knives went into him. Whether intentionally or not, it was a bad hit, and Franz's scream was ear-piercingly loud in the seconds before he broke off for a moment, only to continue screaming.

Suddenly Don found himself possessed of a wrath he hadn't known he was capable of.

He demolished the gang. Every one of them ended up either unconscious or moaning on the ground. His own face and hands cut and bleeding, Don found his younger friend then. He leaned over his friend, panting.

Franz smiled weakly, his thin hands held over the gaping hole in his chest—a rather useless gesture that did nothing to stop the bleeding. The younger boy, temporarily winded from his screaming, couldn't speak. Don's eyes were wide in horror.

"You're..." he breathed in disbelief, taking one of Franz's hands in his own cut ones. Blood trickled from the cuts on Don's hands and face, mingling with the younger boy's.

They could both hear the sirens. Don had learned what the sound meant over the past few weeks. It meant trouble for him and any other gang members.

And even if Don hadn't been a part of the gang, he had a secret terror of the police, anyway.

They could take him away...they could bring him back to the WIPA. And Don had tasted freedom too long to give it up now.

"They're coming." The younger boy's eyes widened. "You should go. They'll take me to a hospital."

"You're sure?" Don bit his lip, aware of how naïve he was and sounded. But he couldn't help that he was completely inexperienced in these sorts of situations.

"Yeah." Franz nodded, wincing. "I'll be fine. I'll see you later. Sometime."

Don forced a smile. "I'll see you, then."

He fled then, making his way out the back of the building and then finding his way through the maze of the docks to escape. In his heart was the vague fear that it would be a long, long time before he saw his younger friend again, if ever.

He had no idea how well-founded that fear was.

* * *

Over the next three years, Don became an experienced inhabitant of the new world he'd found.

He made his own living, whether by performing small jobs for random elderly people or by getting himself accepted into an orphanage until he decided that it was time for him to move on.

He made his way across Europe that way. Being as strong and smart as he was, Don quickly caught on to the habits of the people around him. He became somewhat well-known in certain areas, despite the fact that he attempted to remain hidden—his white suit was still the best clothing he had, and his strength was something far out of the ordinary.

He stayed away from anything WIPA. Even in the WIPA laboratory, Don had known that he was different from most of the other boys: he was stronger, he was smarter, he was faster. Now that revelation was made even more clear. Don was different. Don was unique. Don was...superhuman.

Though he stayed away from WIPA, scientists, and police, Don made a point of being on the lookout for any facts or news about superhumans. There wasn't much information forthcoming; he even went back at some point to investigate the WIPA building he'd come from, only to find that it had been torn down and the space converted into a nuclear power plant. Don discovered nothing about his possible origin or possible destination…until one day when he ventured to make conversation with a young American tourist.

Apparently the American was only too interested in superhumans, and was quite happy to discuss the topic with the curious, young, strong, English-speaking seventeen-year-old porter that carried his suitcases into the Paris hotel. The tourist told Don that superhumans weren't too well-known in Europe…it was more of an American thing.

He also told Don what the boy wanted to know most.

"There's not much fuss about them nowadays. Not in the last year, anyway," the American rambled on, fumbling with his room's key card. "But New York is the place to find them."

"New York?" Don asked, trying not to sound too interested.

"New York City—I'm from there. Thanks for your help… Oh, it was nice talking to you!"

And with that, the twenty-one-year-old, dark brown-haired, deep blue-eyed American headed into his hotel room, taking his suitcase from the younger boy effortlessly and just as effortlessly flinging it onto the bed. Don turned to go, but in the corner of his eye, he saw the name on the luggage tag.

Julien Ransom.

* * *

New York City was just like any other big city, Don decided, after a few hours of initial, tireless wandering. The main difference from any European city was the fact that the people spoke English. Incidentally, English was a language Don happened to know, but he was painfully aware that it was either German-accented or British-accented or both, and that that fact likely made him seem a target for any tourist-spotters, something which Don was determined not to be.

It had been months since he'd run into that American tourist. In the meantime, Don had gotten himself both a passport and a one-way plane ticket to the States. Though he hadn't brought much else besides himself, his trademark white suit, a change of clothes and some supplies from the WIPA base, and some other things that were tucked into his worn backpack, Don felt he was ready to take on New York City. He didn't have money for a hotel, and he didn't really feel like one tonight anyway, so he just kept wandering and accustoming himself to his new surroundings. Eventually dusk fell, and Don realized he was hopelessly lost. Not that he cared. He didn't have a destination, anyway.

At least he didn't until he heard the screaming.

Don had never considered himself a vigilante, but then again he'd never considered himself a bystander, either. Throwing caution to the winds, the young superhuman took off, following his very accurate sense of hearing.

The scene that met his eyes wasn't an unusual one. A gangster-type couple had cornered a girl in a side alley. The girl, probably about nine years old, was shrieking for help. Don was only too eager to provide that help, but he stopped short as a fourth party arrived on the scene, running along some low rooftops and then making a graceful leap down to the pavement, landing easily on both feet and hands. The person allowed himself or herself barely a moment to recover before flipping their body towards the scene of the attempted crime, neatly knocking victim and attackers away from each other.

She had to be a girl, Don realized. The lower half of her face was covered by a tight black mask, and her red hair didn't quite reach her shoulders, but her eyes were definitely feminine. On the left side of her face, her bangs were braided tightly against her head, finally coming to the back where it met the rest of her hair in a bun; on the right side of her face, her bangs hung free almost down to her chin, giving her a rather ruthless, cold look.

She wore a high-collared, dark leather jacket that was somewhat long, going down to about half a foot above her knees and held securely around her waist by an equally dark belt. The jacket had a couple of strangely positioned pockets, and the belt seemed to be of a military type into the bargain—to say nothing of the elbow guards and long black gloves she wore.

Don caught a glimpse of a light purple jacket underneath the leather coat. The girl's somewhat short skirt was black, just as were her tights, knee guards, and high, buckle-less boots. She was probably about twenty years old.

Don was already slowing down as he approached, but now the girl glanced at him briefly before turning her attention back to the gangsters.

"Stand back and watch," she called over her shoulder to the seventeen-year-old. "New York City is my domain."

Don stepped away, gaping as the girl proceeded to give the two gangsters a brief punishment before telling them to clear out or she'd get the police on them again. Helping the little girl to her feet, the masked young woman told the nine-year-old she'd show her home. But Don followed them both.

It was about ten minutes later that the girl had been taken home. The masked stranger took off, but Don ran his fastest to keep up. The way she ran only confirmed the boy's suspicions: this person was also superhuman. And there was something else about her...something gave Don an overwhelming urge to speak to her.

Finally the girl turned, her blue-purple eyes angry. "What do you want?"

"You're a superhuman, aren't you?" Don questioned slowly, breathing hard as he finally caught up to her.

"What should that mean to you?" the girl hissed, tensing. To Don, she looked much like a cat ready to strike.

"Because I am, too," Don went on haltingly. "I came here because—" He broke off as the girl suddenly lunged at him. Don did his best to defend himself, and the two ended up fighting each other hard and fast—it seemed they were a fairly equal match.

Finally, however, the girl managed to pin Don to the concrete ground. He held his breath as he stared into her strangely-colored eyes, eyes that were now filled with confusion.

"You pass the test." Unexpectedly, she helped the seventeen-year-old to his feet. "Who in blazes are you?"

* * *

"So, Miss Knook, do you have any idea why I sent for you?" The WIPA officer stood up to shake the hand of the young woman who'd just entered his office, but it was clear from his greeting that he was very much preoccupied with the task at hand.

"Not really." Eris Knook was about twenty-two years old. Her hair was a light blond, but her bangs had been dyed pink. Her eyes were hazel. Across the underside of her right wrist was a long, thin scar, but there wasn't much else about her that was out of the ordinary. She was dressed in ordinary WIPA officer gear—toned down, of course, since the incident with the Wolf Pack, three and a half years ago.

"Have a seat," the senior officer told her, sitting down himself."So, Miss Knook, I'm sure you've noticed that things have been looking up for WIPA recently."

"Of course," the young woman shrugged. "The commotion about the superhumans has died down, and we've managed to mostly cover up the incident with Lieutenant Anderson, especially as she lost her WIPA status even before that."

"Yes, yes." The man nodded impatiently, tapping his fingers on his desk. "What is your opinion on the current superhuman situation, Eris Knook?"

Eris shrugged again. "They are concentrated in New York City at the present moment. The suspect for Trooper Z has gone off our radar, but there is reason to suspect he, too, is currently making his way to the United States."

"And the Doppelgänger?"

For a moment the young female officer seemed startled. "The Doppelgänger? He's in containment, of course. Why?"

"Do you think he is ready to fulfill his part?" The senior officer seemed slightly amused.

Now Eris openly shuddered. "I wouldn't know. I have nothing to do with him. I only know about him because I'm on the superhuman surveillance team. But I specialize in undercover work in the States."

"I also have heard the rumors that Trooper Z appears to be heading for New York City," the senior officer told her slowly. "If he reaches his destination, it's very likely that he will end up making contact with his family. He may even discover his identity. Naturally, this would be a disaster for the WIPA."

"Mm." Eris nodded slowly.

"I believe it is time for the Doppelgänger to come into the picture." The man leaned back in his chair. "Obviously, he will need to be controlled by someone who knows the lay of the land in NYC."

"You mean *me*, sir?" Eris's eyes opened wide in disbelief. "But I have no experience with handling..."

The officer smiled, handing her an envelope. It was closed, sealed with the WIPA official seal.

"These are your credentials," he told the young officer. "And here is a device that I've sent for from our containment facility. You are to report there for a week of instruction and training. This device will put you in complete control of the Doppelgänger. The envelope also contains your instructions concerning the Whytes."

The man smiled. "No need to look so worried. The Doppelgänger will do the work. Your mission is simple: make superhumans hated by society once again." He paused, his eyes suddenly cold. "And then we can strike again...and we will win."

* * *

It didn't take long for Don and Via to become friends.

She took him home with her that night, introducing herself in the meantime. Don found himself explaining everything he knew about himself to Via's parents: a tall, brown-haired man named Evolet Whyte, and his wife, a red-haired woman with a white streak in her hair, who couldn't seem to believe her eyes.

Via put her toddler siblings, Stanislaus and Lily, to bed. Then she crept back downstairs to listen, highly interested, to what her new acquaintance had to say. Long into the night, Evolet and Scarlet questioned and listened, until the seventeen-year-old was nearly sleeping in his chair. Then Scarlet stood up.

"I'll find you a place to stay," she announced. "And don't make any excuses. You admitted you haven't gotten a place to stay here. And you aren't sleeping in the street."

The tired boy blinked. "But..." he began, then broke off.

Don was dazed, to say the least. To be among other superhumans...to talk to people who were actually intensely interested in him—interested enough to let him spend the night in their home, apparently. It was too much, too suddenly.

Scarlet showed him the room that was usually Julien's, upstairs. Evolet followed the two, and Via stood up and went to make herself a cup of tea. The kitchen was dark and quiet, and she could easily hear her parents' voices as they came downstairs some minutes later.

"We can't be sure, Scar," Evolet was saying quietly. "Don't get your hopes up, please. I know there's a good chance, but I don't want you to be disappointed if he isn't."

"I *know* he is," Scarlet returned obstinately. "It's him. He can't be anyone else. He looks just like you, Evolet! And you think I wouldn't know my own child?"

"Still, we'll get a blood test done tomorrow," Evolet replied. His voice and Scarlet's got quieter as they went past the kitchen, towards the front door. Probably to lock it for the night; it was almost midnight.

Via stood in the kitchen, staring at her tea as she continued stirring it mechanically.

Suddenly she gently let go of the spoon, heading quietly for the stairs. The boy she'd run into was her brother? Via had to see him again.

She eased open the door to the room that was normally her cousin's, and peeked in, holding her breath in hopes that she hadn't awakened the boy—if he was even asleep. To Via's relief, he was. Don's eyes were tightly shut as he lay with his face towards the door. His hair was rumpled, and the moonlight shone through the window upon his strangely peaceful face.

Via watched him a few minutes without making a sound. Don's chest rose and fell lightly, uniformly... Yes, he was definitely asleep.

For the first time, she saw the tattoos on his neck. *Z-021DON*, and then, *WIPA.*

Via caught her breath. So this had to do with WIPA, whether or not "Don" was her younger brother as Scarlet seemed to think he was.

But somehow Via found herself ready to believe it. There was something about Don...something much like a vague nostalgia, that had inclined her from the very beginning to become his friend. She had felt somehow as if she had known him...and now, it seemed, she did.

Via leaned against the door frame sleepily. It seemed forever to her, but it was probably only a few minutes before Scarlet tapped her eldest daughter's shoulder. Via withdrew into the hallway, facing her mother.

"He's asleep?" Scarlet asked, smiling as Via nodded. "Good. Let him sleep. The poor child."

Via let Scarlet lead her towards Via's own room. "Mom, he's one of us, isn't he?"

"Perhaps." Scarlet's voice was unusually quiet. "We'll find out tomorrow."

They had come to Via's room, and Scarlet stood aside to let Via in, but Via turned in the doorway, meeting her mother's eyes. "Mom, what aren't you telling me?"

Scarlet's gaze lowered. "You had a younger brother, Via." As Via didn't react, Scarlet continued: "WIPA took him. You saw him once...and they *took* him. Evolet never met him. I never saw him again. They told me he died."

She paused, her blue eyes alight. "But, Via, I never believed them. And Don... Don might just be that younger brother of yours."

Via was tired, and she felt strange, but she nodded. "I...I hope he is, Mom."

"I do, too."

Suddenly Scarlet hugged her eldest, brushing back Via's short red hair. "Goodnight. You'd better get some sleep. Tomorrow will be a busy day." She lowered the tone of her voice. "So maybe take a break from beating up criminals, eh?"

* * *

The blood test results came back the next afternoon, after Scarlet, Evolet, and Don had blood drawn that morning. Scarlet had been right.

Don was unmistakably and completely a member of the Whyte family.

Scarlet threw a surprise party; Evolet informed all the other Whytes; the spare room became Don's. For a while it seemed as if none of the Whytes could get over the fact that "Conner Aloysius" had been found, and the Whyte parents were no exception. Scarlet didn't want to let her son out of her sight. But gradually, over the course of a month or so, things finally began to settle down once more.

Don became Lily's favorite older brother—forget about Stanislaus. But Stanislaus, too, became one of Don's closest friends. Don discovered that Via's vigilante work was nothing unusual, though he was told nothing about the scars on both sides of her face that were usually covered with makeup, the story behind her very professional combat gear, *or* the reason why she was often quiet and sad-looking. But that last detail prompted Don to try to grow close to her, and he began going out with her on her evening excursions, using his WIPA suit as a bit of a disguise.

Via didn't need the help, but she kindly refrained from telling her younger brother so. The vigilante work became a bond between them, something that knitted them together as best friends and more. Via couldn't help but wonder if things would have been this way if the two had never been separated.

Gradually she began to cheer up and gain a confidence she had never had— except perhaps while she and Eryka had been a superhuman team. Scarlet saw the change in her eldest, and was glad.

But tonight Via was alone, Don having opted to spend the evening helping Scarlet deal with the toddlers—Evolet was working late. Though Via wasn't doing vigilante work tonight. She'd done some errands for Scarlet and was now coming home by subway.

It was late, late enough that Via had no trouble finding an empty seat. She sat down near the back, letting her arms rest from carrying groceries through the streets. She would have to wait on the train for about half an hour before she got to the stop closest to her home—unless she decided to go out and walk or run, an idea that didn't find much favor in Via's mind.

Superhuman though she was, she was somewhat tired. She'd woken up at four in the morning, done a morning job, finished her college courses for the day, completed her homework in record time, and then run free and vigilant through the city until she'd finally settled down long enough to do what Scarlet had asked her "when you get around to it." Via would be happy to fall asleep that night.

Outside, all was darkness; this transport's route ran underground for most of the way. Via let her eyes fall shut, especially as no one was sitting next to her.

Her eyes flew open again some minutes later as the subway abruptly stopped.

They weren't at a station. They had simply stopped in the middle of the dark tunnel. No instructions came across the loudspeaker. Via felt a chill run up her spine.

Then she heard the shouting—and then the screaming. The trouble was further up in the subway.

Via didn't wait long enough to pull up her vigilante mask. Leaving the groceries behind, she stood up and began running through the subway, towards the sounds. She was just getting near when she was thrown to the side of the subway as each of the train cars was rocked by an explosion.

The subway was derailed, falling slowly onto its side. The walls were blackened. People were screaming. Some sort of fire alarm system went off. Via's hands were cut from the glass of the window that had shattered underneath her.

She pulled herself upright, staring around in horror at the people who were screaming. Fire licked one of the seats near the back. The electricity spluttered for a moment and then went out. All was darkness.

Yet Via could see in the dark. And she saw as a lone figure made his way through the train.

His uniform was completely white. It reminded Via of Don's WIPA-inherited gear. But this apparition had a helmet as well. Via could see that the person was a boy about Don's age. His eyes shifted back and forth as he walked, ignoring the chaos and danger around him, looking for—

Via. He saw her just as she realized he was looking for her. With a wild, almost insane shout, the white-dressed attacker sprang towards Via, who was still lying on what had once been the side of the subway car.

They made contact. Via met him fighting and she kept on fighting. A few minutes of intense combat followed, in which Via found herself horribly pressed and desperate. She could fight, that was for sure. She could hold her own. That was equally true. But when her opponent seemed possessed of an almost rabid obstinacy, and kept screaming wordlessly at her— It was unsettling.

He pulled out a knife, lunging forward. The blade was stopped by Via's purple jacket, but that didn't prevent her from being winded. Via grabbed the blade and tried to jerk it away, but her opponent let go after only an instant, and Via stumbled backwards. She was slammed against the wall—formerly the floor—a moment later as her opponent knocked her forward.

She ducked away as he came hurtling forward, and leapt for his back, knife in hand. But his white suit was strangely blade-resistant, much like Via's own jacket, and the knife was knocked away as the struggle continued.

Suddenly Via found herself facing another knife, but this time the steel came for her throat.

Her collar only half-blocked it, and Via was knocked to the floor. She kicked upwards as the attacker, his suit now worn and bloodstained, leapt forward; but that held him off for only a moment. The next second he had pinned her to the ground, his hands closing around her neck as he laughed madly, triumphantly.

Via tried to strike back, but he was just as strong as her, if not stronger, and she couldn't breathe and was bleeding badly. She tried to pull his hands away, but failed as she found herself getting weaker and weaker. As her own fingers tightened, so did his. Via began gagging, staring up at the unnaturally black eyes of her opponent.

She was passing out, she realized. Her head was pounding...and she still couldn't breathe.

She needed air. Her vision was strange... She could hear him laughing still. Laughing in a crazy, deranged voice.

But suddenly the sound broke off as the boy lifted his head, listening intently for a moment to whatever was coming through his earpiece. His face broke into a scowl. Angrily, he let go of Via and stood up as yet more explosions rocked the subway and suddenly the entire car burst into flame.

Taking a moment longer to hit the side of Via's face, so hard that the makeup she wore came off on his gloves, the boy stepped away, breaking the window above them both with one hard blow and then pulling himself up through it. A moment later, he had gone.

Via wouldn't have believed her eyes…if she had been conscious. She coughed a bit as she began to breathe again, but her eyes didn't open. She lay, limp and deserted, as the flames slowly surrounded her…

* * *

Lights. Voices. A steady beeping.

Via could remember places like this before. But in none of them had she felt this strange, heavy darkness that weighed her mind down. She felt her forehead wrinkle as she came fully conscious, but she didn't open her eyes. Now she felt someone's hand take her own, and she sighed involuntarily.

Her neck hurt, her face hurt…her entire body hurt. But that wasn't why Via didn't want to wake up.

"Via? Can you hear me now?"

It was her mother's voice.

Reluctantly, Via finally opened her eyes. She could see Scarlet, Evolet, Julien, Don… They were around the hospital bed. But instead of looking at them, Via's eyes focused on the white ceiling. It was so white…so horribly white.

It wasn't the ceiling. It was the light that was blinding her, Via realized. She winced.

"Via," Evolet spoke up. "How do you feel?"

"I'm alive," Via breathed as the realization finally hit her. Her eyes widened in horror as she remembered. The screaming, the flames…the white-clad superhuman.

"You're alive." Evolet smiled weakly. "You're…you're the lucky survivor, girl. You're burnt, and cut, and bruised, but yes, you're alive. What happened?"

He bit his lip. "Also, I think the police want to talk to you—"

"I want to go home," Via interrupted suddenly, still staring starkly at the ceiling.

"I do, too..." Evolet's smile faded as he realized Via wasn't joking.

She began shaking, shutting her eyes tightly. A policeman came over to the bedside, and Scarlet stood up.

"Not now," she murmured firmly, her eyes narrowed. "I'll contact you when she's ready."

She glanced back at her daughter, and Scarlet's gaze fell.

Via was in bad shape—it was a miracle she was still alive.

But what scared Scarlet most was her daughter's face.

Via's claw scars—on both cheeks, ever since the incident with Diana Anderson—were fully visible, but that wasn't what concerned Scarlet. No, it was the look she had seen in her daughter's eyes. Confusion, fear...and something very much like disappointment.

But Via would have to recover herself soon, Scarlet realized. The entire city was in an uproar about the subway accident. Via was the only survivor. And no one knew the cause...

And Scarlet was well aware that fingers were already being pointed at her daughter as the prime suspect.

* * *

Yet it was an entire week before Via could be persuaded to talk. And even then, that was only because the attacks on the city had continued. Now Via's narration of the disaster was accepted as plausible...but it didn't help the police to stop the terror.

The white killer was somewhere one moment and another place the next. He was superhuman, the police knew that much. He seemed to have been specifically trained and designed for killing; they knew that, too. But that was the limit of their knowledge. And there was no stopping the criminal.

Meanwhile, Via did not recover.

She spent her time alone in her room, sitting or lying in her bed with the curtains drawn. She barely ate. She didn't speak unless spoken to, and then only in short sentences or even single words. In her eyes was a live, real, overwhelming fear. But what was worse than the fear was the horror and disappointment.

It scared Scarlet. The only explanation she could think of was that Via was disappointed that she had survived...and Scarlet naturally didn't want her daughter to be thinking that way. She did her best to comfort Via, to calm her, but nothing seemed to accomplish anything. Via still lay awake at night, her eyes open wide as she stared at the ceiling. Scarlet feared for her sanity.

Meanwhile, the white-clad boy reigned over New York City. He seemed to target places frequented by the Whytes, but apparently he didn't know where the Whytes lived, so they managed to keep out of the way.

Until one day when Conner ran into him.

It wasn't intentional. Conner wasn't usually out and about in the city, much preferring to spend his free time somewhere out in the country. He liked to consider himself retired. But when the worst came to worst, Conner was just as ready as anyone else to fight—and to fight hard.

He was in a grocery store when the terrorist-style attack began, out in the parking lot. Conner happened to be nearby household supplies at the time, and he didn't lose a second in grabbing a couple of fire extinguishers and making a dash for the store entrance. Just as he'd suspected, the disturber was none other than the "White Killer," as the teenage boy was now known as in the city.

Conner got out of the doorway quickly—most of the people that had been in the parking lot were now rushing his way for shelter. Conner couldn't help but notice the way the White Killer's face lit up when the boy caught sight of the older, yet somehow perpetually young Whyte adult. Conner tore off one of the extinguisher's safety seal and wrapped his hand around the trigger as the White Killer leapt towards him, ready for action.

Conner stood firm and unwavering as the boy came flying through the air. Unflinching, Conner waited until the instant just before the collision to let fly with the extinguisher's contents.

As always, the former Violet Army soldier's aim was perfect, and Conner sidestepped unnoticed, the White Killer's helmet visor having been completely covered with white foam. Wielding the fire extinguisher with his usual superhuman strength, Conner smashed the metal canister against the side of the White Killer's helmet.

As the boy reeled momentarily, Conner grabbed hold of him, slamming him down on the pavement with the same kind of ruthless energy he'd so often wielded in the Violet Army. He was well aware that he'd need every scrap of experience he had to defeat this new enemy.

He had the boy on the ground now. Conner knew he wouldn't be able to defeat the younger superhuman while the White Killer was still fully protected by his white gear, but that was only a matter of time. Working quickly, Conner tore off the boy's helmet, revealing the boy's face and most of his neck.

Shockingly, the boy's eyes were just as black without the mask as they were with it. He seemed even angrier and crazier than usual, his mouth nearly foaming as he screamed in pure hatred at the older veteran. And even still, Conner did notice the tattoos on the side of the White Killer's neck.

Z-022GAN.

WIPA.

"Give up!" Conner shouted, wincing momentarily as the boy's fist crashed into Conner's own, unprotected face.

His suggestion was met with more screaming. Suddenly Conner found the tables turned as the White Killer struck out with all his available energy, finally succeeding in gaining the upper hand.

The White Killer didn't even bother to use the knife at his belt. Now that he could see again, he seemed intent on beating the older man to unconsciousness and perhaps even death.

Conner fought back as well as he could, but the White Killer, too, had had military training, and besides that, the boy's strain of T4 seemed to be like Via's—well-known in the Whyte circle to be the most powerful of all superhuman strains. Added to that was the boy's overwhelmingly insane determination. Conner felt horribly that he was fighting a wild animal.

Suddenly, amid the blows that flew back and forth, Conner became aware of a voice that was coming through the White Killer's helmet. The words that were spoken were in German, and the White Killer paused a moment to listen.

Conner was almost certain that the words were a command to fall back—like they'd been with Via—but then the White Killer picked up the helmet and used it to try to smash Conner's face in.

The next seconds that passed were crazy ones.

Somehow Conner managed to break away, and once he did, he got up and started running. He didn't stop until he was sure he had left the White Killer behind. Only then did he collapse against a wall, panting harder than he'd ever breathed in his life, feeling the pain from his cuts and bruises for the first time.

Eventually he found the strength to stand up again. Slowly and carefully, Conner began limping in the direction of Evolet and Scarlet's house.

* * *

"The boy is a monster," Conner was saying quietly later that evening, as Scarlet made him a cup of coffee, having already taken the time to bandage her father-in-law's face. "He has to be insane. There is no other explanation."

"That still doesn't explain where he comes from," Evolet sighed, glancing over at the windows that had recently been covered with blackout curtains.

"No," Conner shook his head. "But there is something that might."

"What is it?" Scarlet questioned from the other end of the kitchen.

"You know the letters and numbers on the side of our Don's neck?" Conner began heavily. "His WIPA ID? Well, the White Killer has an ID that's much the same. The only difference is that the White Killer's combination reads 'Z-022GAN.'"

"Could Gan be part of his name?" Evolet wondered after a moment. "Like Don's... Or just his entire name. We wouldn't know."

"His name doesn't matter," Scarlet broke in sharply, and Conner nodded agreement.

"Besides that, there are other developments," the older adult went on. "If you ask me, the White Killer has been taking orders from someone. I don't know who, but my first guess would be WIPA."

"The monsters," Evolet hissed, and this time no one bothered to disagree with him.

"The problem is, if he is taking orders, he's now begun to disobey those orders." Conner sighed heavily. "I'm ninety percent sure that he was ordered not to kill me earlier. He paused for a moment and then attacked me with his helmet. I think he destroyed the communication system in the process."

"Great," Evolet scowled. "So now there's a maniac killer loose in New York City, and not even his already murderous owners have power over him anymore."

"I'd make the comparison to a mad dog off his leash," Conner nodded. "The point remains. This is a bad situation. And, of course, we Whytes are the only ones who can do anything about it, apparently."

"What a mess," Scarlet sighed. "And, unfortunately, I think you're right. We're going to have to be the ones to clean it up."

"Those WIPA," Evolet muttered. "After this, I'm going to find their new headquarters, wherever it is, and tell them publicly what I think of them." His purple eyes were hard and angry. "They should be in prison. Each and every one of them."

"The question is, what are we going to do now?" Scarlet reminded her husband gently.

"Julien's already here," Evolet reasoned. "I guess we'll need all the help we can get. Should I call Jaz and see if she's free to stay here a week or two? Or should we all split up?"

"Tell her to come here," Conner advised. "Moira and I are nearby if you need us. But if Jaz is on the other side of the city, she might not be in time to help if anything happens."

"Right." Evolet stood up, fishing around in his pocket for his phone. "We'll do that, then."

In the meantime, Scarlet handed the mug of coffee to her father-in-law. He smiled his thanks.

"Don't tell Moira, but I always did think you were the best in the family at making coffee," he admitted, and Scarlet laughed for a moment before her face grew serious once again.

"I'll be back in a moment," she promised. "I'm just going to check on Via."

"The poor girl," Conner sighed. "Yes, do. The other kids are asleep, aren't they?"

"Yes," Scarlet returned shortly as she left the room and marched quietly towards the stairs.

As usual, she knocked gently before opening the door to her eldest daughter's room, but there was no response. Tiptoeing in, Scarlet was happily surprised to see that Via actually seemed to be asleep. She would have left the room without a moment's delay if she hadn't just then seen the small bottle that stood on the nightstand.

A sudden fear struck her, and she quickly and quietly made her way over to the bed, leaning over Via and listening carefully. Relieved, Scarlet saw that her daughter was still breathing. She turned and picked up the bottle, reading the label swiftly. Her eyes widened, and she caught her breath as she read it a second time.

It was a suppressant for "hypersthenodynamosomatosis." Being the scientist she was, Scarlet didn't have to ponder long before she realized what was going on.

The bottle was a suppressant for T7, presumably the same drug that Via had taken during all the years the girl had lived with her aunt and uncle.

Scarlet shook her head in disbelief, slipping the bottle into her pocket. Why would Via be taking a T7 suppressant? Scarlet had long ago heard all the miseries of the drug. It made the user sick, depressed, tired... It was a mild form of Eternity Schwann's "cure."

Scarlet sat down softly by her daughter's side, running her hand across Via's warm forehead. Via stirred, her scarred face contorting for a moment as she murmured something in her sleep. Then the lines straightened themselves out again, and Via's face was peaceful once more. Scarlet brushed Via's short hair out of the younger girl's face...Via seemed to have given up on letting her hair grow long ever since it had been cut short by Diana Anderson a year and a half ago.

The mother felt tears sting her eyes. Her heart bled for her eldest daughter. Via's childhood had been a nightmare... The incident with Via's old best friend, Eryka Ulven, had been even worse. There had been a year or so of peace, during which Via's tightly imprisoned soul had slowly opened up to the world around her…

Then there was Diana Anderson's attack on the family, in which the WIPA Lieutenant had drugged and used Via to try to kill Via's own family. And now…the trauma of being nearly killed—though Scarlet suspected that, for Via, the trauma was more that of having been the only survivor.

Scarlet brushed away her tears before they could disturb the sleeper. More than ever before, Scarlet wished that she could help Via… But it was during times like these that Scarlet fully realized how far apart she was from her daughter. No one was close to Via, let alone her mother Scarlet, who'd been in an asylum for nearly fifteen years of Via's life. No, Scarlet had been away from her daughter too long.

There was a slight chance that Eryka could have been the friend Via had needed…but now Eryka was gone, after having betrayed the younger redhead twice before trying to kill her.

Now Via tried to be kind to her family—she had no friends—but there was a part of her that was always locked away, that no one could ever reach. Now, it seemed, Via had withdrawn entirely into that cocoon, and no one could call her out of it.

"Via," Scarlet whispered, unable to contain herself. "Via…I love you."

She held her daughter's hand, and squeezed it, but Via's face showed no sign of recognition. Sighing, Scarlet stood up and left the room, taking the drug with her. She would not let Via hurt herself further.

But that wasn't the only resolution that Scarlet came away with. No, she had another goal in mind.

Scarlet would find and capture, or otherwise incapacitate, the White Killer. She would put an end to the maniac's reign of terror, and do it herself, somehow—there was no need to endanger anyone else. She would do it so that Via would fear no longer.

This would be the *last* attack WIPA would make upon the Whytes.

Scarlet was determined that no one would hurt her daughter, never again.

* * *

"Yeah, yeah, I'll talk to you later, Gwen." Julien smiled as he waved a goodbye to his phone camera. "It was nice seeing you again!"

Ending the call abruptly, Julien stood, glancing up at his uncle Evolet. "What's up?"

"That was Gwen?" Evolet raised his eyebrows slightly.

The young man shrugged. "The Wolf told me to look out for her. That was before the Wolf went and got herself killed, remember? Of course, Gwen's got her own family now, but still...But what's wrong?"

"I was just wondering if you'd seen Scarlet," Evolet questioned slowly, running a hand through his thick brown hair.

"Aunt Scarlet? No, I haven't," Julien realized. "What, is she missing?"

"Maybe." Evolet sighed. "What a life, man. What a life."

* * *

"Don't go in there." The young woman stepped directly into Scarlet's path, blocking the store entrance. Her voice was layered with a light German accent. "You won't make it out alive. The police are already on their way."

Scarlet's blue eyes narrowed into slits. "Get out of my way. The police won't accomplish anything."

"Neither will you, Mrs. Whyte," the woman went on, and this time Scarlet gave her a good look.

The stranger was dressed in semi-military-style clothes, which Scarlet now recognized as being rather WIPA-ish. Her bangs and hair tips were dyed a light blue, but the rest of her hair was light blond. Her eyes were hazel. Across her right wrist was a thin, yet distinct scar. Scarlet's eyebrows shot up.

"How do you know who I am?" she demanded frankly.

The young woman held out her hand, obviously prepared to handshake. "The name's Eris Knook. I'm from WIPA."

Scarlet took the hand, but she didn't shake it. Instead, she twisted it slightly and jerked Eris out of her way, holding her against the wall of a nearby building. "You're from WIPA?" she demanded, her voice dangerously soft as her eyes glinted cold and hard.

Eris winced at the sudden pain as her arm was twisted.

"Y—yes," she nodded, feeling her heart rate increase dramatically. "I've been wanting to meet you—"

She let out a sharp cry of pain as Scarlet twisted the WIPA officer's arm again, bringing her to her knees this time. "You'd better start talking," the redhead hissed angrily.

"Yes, yes," Eris murmured, her face white. "I'll talk, alright. No force is necessary. —You want me to talk *here?*"

Scarlet glanced around, becoming aware of the sound of approaching sirens for the first time. She bit her lip.

"No. I'm going to take you home with me, Miss Knook. And don't try anything or I'll show you what I'd like to do to every one of you sickening WIPA."

* * *

"I don't think I need to tell you that we want to hear every detail," Evolet told Eris slowly, about half an hour later. "Every detail, Miss Knook."

Eris sighed for what seemed to her the millionth time. "I know, I know," she muttered as she sat down in the seat that had been pointed out to her. "Don't worry about it. You do realize I effectively lost all WIPA status the moment I made contact with Mrs. Whyte?"

Evolet ignored the comment. "Who is the White Killer?"

"He was born Dirk Zeidler," Eris recited quietly. "His WIPA ID is Z-022GAN, and his code-name is Doppelgänger. Known to trainees and comrades as Gänger, he was raised in the same facility as your son Don." The WIPA officer glanced over at the seventeen-year-old, who stared unblinkingly back.

"What is he, and why is he superhuman?" Scarlet wanted to know.

"He is a beta tester." Eris sounded as if she were quoting her instruction classes word-for-word. "He was raised and trained to be a Doppelgänger Whyte. His mission? To destroy the superhuman reputation."

"And where do you come in?" Conner's eyes were narrowed. Leaning back in her chair, Eris told them everything.

She told them of how she had been a street thief in Berlin, spending time in and out of prison before ending up in WIPA hands when she was nineteen—three years ago.

Faced with apparently perpetual imprisonment, Eris had attempted suicide, a shocking gesture which had brought her case to the attention of the higher-up WIPA officials.

After some debate, they'd decided to offer Eris a chance: she could become a WIPA officer, and, in return, regain her freedom and gain a reputation and identity she had never had in the first place. Naturally, Eris had accepted.

Despite, and perhaps because of, her strange background, Eris hadn't been involved in anything big—until now. Now, she told the Whytes, she had been assigned the job of managing the Doppelgänger in New York City. Her orders were to spread terror and initiate distrust for all superhumans among the general population. That was why she had been instructed not to let the Doppelgänger kill any Whytes—not yet.

"That was where WIPA went wrong," Eris continued unflinchingly. "The Doppelgänger was trained to hate all Whytes with every fiber of his being. And, in the end, that hatred was too strong to be held back." The WIPA officer glanced at Conner. "That was when he disobeyed me—and tried to kill you."

"So now this superhuman lunatic is running free, completely unrestrained, in New York City," Jasmine surmised, her eyes narrowed. "And that's all you have to say."

"Yes." Eris nodded, then fell silent, dropping her gaze to her hands in her lap. Jasmine caught her breath as she saw Eris trace the scar across the WIPA's wrist gently, while a slightly absent expression crept over Eris's face.

"You ought to go to the police," Scarlet muttered, and Jasmine glanced at her in disbelief.

"Yes, yes," Eris breathed simply.

Evolet bit his lip. "What aren't you telling us?" he fairly shouted.

Finally the WIPA glanced up at him, her hazel eyes devoid of any emotion. "I've told you everything I know. It's up to you to catch and defeat that monster now."

"I think I agree with you about the police, Scarlet," Conner put in finally.

"So do I," Eris nodded.

Julien's eyebrows shot up. "How are you so fine with that?" he demanded in frank astonishment.

Eris shrugged lightly. "What else would you do with me? You know just as well as I do that I'm partly responsible for letting the Doppelgänger loose. I'd expect nothing else but to be taken to the police."

Suddenly, abruptly, Jasmine stepped forward, smiling slightly as she locked eyes with the WIPA.

"Maybe we'll take you to the police after all this is over," she murmured quietly, and everyone else glanced at her in surprise. "But for now, I think it's better that we keep you with us. There's no need to go and try to kill yourself again, yet, is there?" Jasmine shook her head. "Better stick around for now, Miss Knook. Yes?"

* * *

"I don't see why you thought we could keep a better eye on her than the police could," Evolet muttered to his sister, shaking his head annoyedly. "Look at us now, leaving her behind at the house while we set off to find the Doppelgänger and defeat him by sheer weight of numbers. I don't call that safe."

"That's why Don and Via are at home," Jasmine replied smoothly, keeping up the pace as she and the other Whyte adults marched down the street. "And that's why we left Stan and Lily with Aunt Moira. It'll be alright."

"If you say so," Evolet growled, obviously unconvinced. "Well, let's hope we find the Doppelgänger today. I don't like this plan of simply wandering around until we run into trouble."

* * *

"Via," Don called into the darkness of his older sister's room, "can you watch Eris for a bit? I just want to run down the street and get us all a snack, okay?"

"Hang on," came Via's soft response. Surprisingly enough, her voice was coming from the restroom. Don bit his lip as he smelled something suspicious.

"Via, you didn't just throw up, did you?"

"It's nothing!" His sister's voice was unusually snappish. "Go get your snack. Don't get anything for me, though."

"You'll keep an eye on Eris?" Don asked hopefully.

"I will. Just go away," Via shouted.

Don sighed. "Fine. Whatever. Bye."

Heading downstairs, the seventeen-year-old ran into Eris. "I'm going to pop outside for a minute," he told the older young woman briefly. "Hey, can you please check on my sister? I don't think she's doing well."

"Your sister Via?" Eris raised her eyebrows. "Alright, I'll do that."

"Thanks," Don returned, heading for the front door.

Eris made her way upstairs, eventually finding Via's room by means of trial and error. "Miss Whyte?" she called softly, seeing that no one was in the bed.

Suddenly Via stepped out of the restroom, glancing blankly towards the doorway of her room. "Oh...it's you."

"Are you alright?" Eris questioned simply, raising her eyebrows.

"You're WIPA, aren't you?" Via's question was more like a statement. "Stay away from me."

Eris held up her hands defensively. "I'm not trying to hurt you, Via Whyte. Can we talk this over?" she asked diplomatically.

She couldn't help but notice how blank and white Via's scarred face was. No wonder Don had been worried about his sister. Perhaps Eris was vaguely worried as well. Perhaps not.

"There's nothing to talk about." Via sat down on her bed, leaning against the far wall and closing her eyes. "Goodnight."

"It's two in the afternoon." Eris laughed shortly.

"Might as well be two in the morning," the redhead muttered, clearly uninterested in continuing any conversation with the former officer.

Abruptly, Eris gave up. "Well, goodbye," she retorted, turning and walking away. She left Via's door open behind her, but that was more of an accident, as Eris had suddenly become distracted by a voice downstairs.

But it wasn't a voice. It was a laugh. And not a Whyte's laugh, but a cold, wild, hysterical laugh Eris knew only too well. She felt her blood run cold.

So the Doppelgänger had found the house. And Eris was there, with no one but a semi-conscious Via for company.

The young officer had frozen still for a moment, but somehow she managed to pluck up the courage to rethink the situation. She could call the Whytes. That might accomplish something. But it would also lead the Doppelgänger towards the stairs, and he might discover Via, in which case all hell would break loose.

Or Eris could go downstairs and try to make the Doppelgänger obey her once again. Only a couple of days had passed since she'd lost control, after all. Perhaps she could contain the menace...and perhaps then there would be a chance for her.

Ignoring the cold terror it gave her, Eris chose her second option.

She went quietly, slowly down the stairs, wincing as she saw how hard her hands were shaking. "This won't do," she whispered to herself to try to calm her own nerves. "This won't do at *all*, Eris Knook!"

Then she turned the corner of the staircase, only to see the Doppelgänger standing there at the foot of the stairs, watching her. He'd heard even the small sounds Eris had made in her descent, it seemed.

Eris took a deep breath, holding tightly to the railing.

"Doppelgänger," she spoke out, though her voice was perhaps a little too quiet. It got louder as the Doppelgänger didn't move and Eris regained a speck of confidence. "Don't you move."

He held still, watching Eris as she began to descend the last few steps.

Then the spell was broken as the mad superweapon's unavoidable hatred for his masters and trainers broke loose and rampaged over his initial fear. The WIPA was just a human, after all. How could *she* stand in his way?

Eris's scream was broken short as the Doppelgänger slammed her back up to the stairs' landing. Eris heard and felt something snap as she hit the wall—a rib, she guessed starkly. Maybe two.

"Stop it!" she shouted in one last desperate attempt to regain control. But all control had been permanently lost.

The Doppelgänger dropped back for a moment as Eris braced herself against the pain that swept through her, trying to pull herself back up the higher half of the staircase.

The boy's empty, black, unlit eyes burned in pure hatred as he watched her a moment, panting. He knew WIPA, only too well. They had bred him to hate, to kill...

But, most of all, they had tried to hold him back.

Unforgivable.

He followed Eris up the steps, noticing with a strangely satisfying delight that the WIPA was afraid...no, terrified. In turn, Eris's hazel eyes opened wider as she stumbled backwards up the steps, nearly bent double from the pain in her chest.

She tripped over the last step, and fell forward with a scream. But the Doppelgänger chose that moment to pounce. Eris's foot twisted as she was knocked backwards onto the upstairs floor, the Doppelgänger at her throat.

With an unearthly, triumphant scream, the boy reached for one of the knives at his belt with his free hand. But he never finished the motion, suddenly realizing that Eris in turn was trying to pull a device out of her pocket.

A tiny spark of fear flickered in the maniac's eyes, and he jerked the device away from Eris, throwing it away, far away. The next moment, his tightly clenched fists hit Eris's face simultaneously. Eris screamed once again, and this time the Doppelgänger succeeded in gaining a hold on one of his knives.

It was all over from then on, really. Eris didn't have any protective clothing like Via's or the Doppelgänger's. It was only a matter of seconds before she and her clothes were drenched in blood and she was passing out. Then again, the Doppelgänger wasn't targeting anything vital. It was almost as if, in his own savage way, he wanted Eris to suffer.

But then, strangely enough, the Doppelgänger paused and looked up.

"Come on and get me, Whyte Killer," a new voice drawled. It was Via's voice.

The Doppelgänger seemed to be indecisive for a moment, but then he picked himself up, staring across the short distance to Via. Unlike his hatred for his trainers, the Doppelgänger's hatred for every member of the Whyte family had been built and fostered in him as strongly as his combat instincts.

"You'd better be ready to do something, WIPA," Via went on, and she coughed. "Because I'm going to last about five seconds."

That was as far as she got before the Doppelgänger took the bait and leapt towards his new enemy.

Eris was bleeding, gasping for breath, passing out. She was done. But the realization seemed to awake in her that, somehow, Via had decided to draw the Doppelgänger away from the WIPA. Why, Eris didn't know. It was too late, anyway.

But Eris did know one thing that could possibly save the Whyte girl.

The device that had been given to her by her WIPA superior. The device that was supposedly connected to some chip inside the Doppelgänger's suit that would somehow temporarily electrocute him.

The Doppelgänger knew about it. That was why he had knocked the device away from Eris. But now the Doppelgänger had left her alone.

Eris forced herself to roll over once, then twice, though every movement doubled her pain. Then, even as Via's hoarse scream rang out, Eris couldn't roll over anymore. No, her energy was gone...

The device was still so far away.

Could she reach it?

Desperately, Eris crept her bloody hand along the floor, reaching, straining... Finally her fingers closed around it.

Eris lost no time in pressing the button as hard as she could. This time it was the Doppelgänger who screamed: a horrifying, chilling sound. And then, wonder of wonders...

He turned tail and fled. Down the stairs, out of the house, away.

Eris turned her head, seeing the bleeding, beaten Via leaning against the wall. Eris couldn't help a snort of disgust.

"What'd you do that for?" she demanded, her voice weak and faint, and her German accent much stronger than usual.

"He was killing you," Via coughed, her eyes falling shut.

"He's already killed me," Eris returned. "What about you? What's wrong with you, Via Pacis Whyte?"

And then Via opened her eyes. "I don't want to be superhuman anymore," she whispered. In her blue-purple eyes was the darkness of calm despair. "I am tired...so tired...of surviving."

"You think you have a choice?"

Via glanced at the WIPA in surprise as Eris coughed blood, trying to recover herself to speak again.

"You think you have the option to abandon your strength?"

She shook her head in disgust. "I know you better than you know yourself, Via Whyte, and I'm telling you you have no right to be *weak!*"

Via started, her eyes wide. She half-stood up.

Then Eris's eyes fell shut as she coughed one last time and then stopped breathing.

Via felt the officer's wrist for a pulse in vain. Eris would not open her eyes again.

The redheaded Whyte straightened, leaning against the wall as she coughed into her hand. She opened her fist then, not too surprised to see that she had coughed blood. Via felt bruised and battered... But, she realized suddenly, she wasn't broken.

No, she wasn't broken, and she wasn't going to break. Perhaps she was still under some of the suppressant drug's effects, but she was still alive. She was alive, just as she had been alive for the past twenty years.

And now wasn't the time to be giving up.

Via glanced up, her eyes alight with a newly regained hope. Despite the blood that covered her, and the scars on her face, and the bruise that was forming on her cheek, Via looked more alive than she had in over a week. Slowly she straightened, but not until she had picked up the device that had fallen out of Eris's grip.

She made her way downstairs, her face determined and her jaw hard-set. Via was going to find the Doppelgänger. And this time, she would defeat him.

* * *

Whatever Don might have been expecting to see upon his return, it was definitely not the scene that actually met his eyes.

The boy spent almost half a minute staring at Eris's limp form. He wasn't too horrified—Don had seen the worst of two continents at this point—but he *was* shocked. Don finally bent down to feel for a pulse, but found none. The body was already growing cold.

Struck by a sudden fear, Don pulled his phone out of his pocket and dialed his parents' number as he ran towards his sister's room, looking around wildly. She was nowhere to be seen. Quickly Don moved to search the other rooms.

"Don? What's wrong?" It was his father's voice.

"I'm sorry, Dad." Don's voice was strangely shaky, the boy realized, and he tried to keep it under control. "I...I left the house. I just got back and..." Don bit his lip. Via wasn't anywhere upstairs.

"What happened?" Evolet demanded sharply.

"Miss Knook is dead," Don admitted, holding the railing tightly as he went down the stairs. "I...I don't think it was a suicide, Dad." The seventeen-year-old swallowed hard.

"And Via?"

"I can't find her anywhere."

Evolet took a moment to confer with the other adults, and then he came back to the call. "Don? You still there?"

"Yes," Don answered quickly.

"Are there any signs that the Doppelgänger was there?"

Don could feel his knees shaking. "I—I don't know." His voice got a lot quieter as he realized there was a chance the Doppelgänger could still be in the vicinity. Don backed himself up against the wall of the living room, glancing around with fearful eyes. "I don't think he's still here now, if he was. But Via isn't anywhere."

Evolet paused a moment, then issued his instructions. "Okay...I don't know what's going on. Your mother and Julien are going to head over now. But get yourself out of the danger area. And... See if you can find out where Via went."

"Okay, Dad." Suddenly another, almost more horrible fear struck the boy. "Dad, you don't think Via did it, do you?"

"I don't," Evolet muttered. "But... She could be in danger. I'll talk to you again soon, Don."

"See you, Dad."

Don stared at his phone as Evolet hung up, and the seventeen-year-old took a deep breath, heading towards the front door. So he had to find Via? Well, she couldn't have gone far, could she? But there was an easier way to find her. If she had her phone on her.

Don glanced at the tracker map on his phone screen. He could see Evolet's location, Scarlet's, and...Via's.

"Central Park?" he muttered. "What does she want at Central Park? Oh, blast, it's starting to rain."

* * *

"That's right," Via murmured to herself, risking a brief glance behind her to see the white-clad figure that was tearing after her. "Keep on coming, Whyte Killer!"

What with her loss of blood and now her racing heart, Via's system had already begun to do some damage to the suppressant she'd taken some hours before. Now her body began to come alive again, and the light in her eyes grew stronger as she pedaled at her fastest speed through the streets of New York City.

Already having been shouted at by several policemen, Via simply kept going, dodging traffic and leaving any possible collisions to affect her pursuer instead of her. But somehow the "White Killer" kept coming as well, becoming surprisingly adept at city survival, though Via was obviously much better at it than the lab-trained superweapon.

And as Via had told Don when they first met, New York City was her domain.

She was completely decked out in the combat suit she'd retained from her brief stay with Lieutenant Diana Anderson. Covered from head to toe in bulletproof, blade-proof material, Via would not be falling as easily as she had in her first encounter with the Doppelgänger, though she was still weaker than usual. No, this time Via was as ready to rampage as was the monster himself.

Finally she reached her destination: New York City's Central Park. Via ignored all possible rules and restrictions and pedaled right through the gate, through the grass, and beyond. Behind her came the white avenger. Via's bike was slowed by the grass, and she fumbled for the shocker device at her belt. Her hand closed around it just as her bicycle hit a rock. The bike flew into the air, but Via was already leaping off it. She hit the ground rolling, and recovered herself in seconds, while the Doppelgänger came within view once again.

He was running hard and fast, especially now that Via had stopped. In unconscious imitation of her grandfather's technique a few days before, Via stood ready and waiting for the enemy to approach her across the grassy lawn. Her fingers were wrapped securely around the device again.

"So tired of fighting," Via breathed, her eyes cold and hard. "This is not going to happen again!"

For the second time in the past month, the Doppelgänger rushed towards Via, leaping into the air for the first few feet.

Via smiled grimly, held her ground, and hit the button as she sidestepped at the last second.

The Doppelgänger hit the ground where Via had been standing a moment before. He was screaming from the instant Via hit the button, however. But even then Via didn't hesitate to let the button go and hit it again, right before she pulled out her handgun—another legacy from Diana—and shot twice.

She missed. Her hands were shaky, and the Doppelgänger was recovering faster than Via had reckoned for. Panting, the redhead kept on shooting as he came at her, but none of the bullets found their way past his suit. Then she was out of ammunition.

He knocked her down, and Via felt the breath go out of her, but she kept her eyes open. "Not again!" she shouted, while the Doppelgänger roared back in answer.

She threw the gun hard at his exposed face. She had planned to scramble back to her feet and run until she could figure out what to do next, but just then a familiar voice interrupted her thoughts.

"Via! Via, are you—"

Via never heard the rest of Don's question; she half-flipped over in the split second before the Doppelgänger landed. This time, Via beat the maniac at his own game, snatching a knife out of the Doppelgänger's own belt. She lunged for his face. The Doppelgänger half-recoiled, but then he grabbed the blade in his own gloved hands and twisted it—and Via's arm, in the process. Then, since she didn't let go, the Doppelgänger half-yanked Via to her feet and then slammed her against a nearby light post.

That was all he had time for before Don landed on the Doppelgänger's back.

It seemed this was a fight they had fought in the past. Both boys were equally well-matched; both were wearing similarly protective clothing. Don found himself laughing back at the maniacal laughter of the Doppelgänger.

"You remember, hey, Gänger?" Don shouted at his opponent in German. "You remember! Do you remember that I always won?"

He landed a hard hit to the Doppelgänger's face, which was returned in like kind. Fists flew between them, and it was an equal battle until Via rejoined the fight.

"Via!" Don shouted in surprise.

"Don't pay attention to me—let's win this!" Via sounded just as determined as her younger brother.

And then, unexpectedly, the Doppelgänger broke away.

He pulled himself free and began running, fast and then faster. Don and Via stared at each other in shock for a moment before taking off in pursuit. They couldn't let the killer get away, or nothing would have been accomplished.

Panicking, the Doppelgänger fled for his life and freedom, out of Central Park and back into the streets. Don and Via were doing their best to keep up when a car suddenly slammed directly into the White Killer and two adults leapt out. Julien Ransom and Scarlet Whyte.

Screaming something in German, the Doppelgänger hesitated for barely a moment before throwing himself at Scarlet. He was only trying to get away at this point, but Scarlet was already aware of the situation, and she grabbed hold of the boy's arm even as she was shoved roughly against the windshield. The glass of the window cracked; Scarlet fell backwards, pulling the Doppelgänger with her.

He pulled his other knife free and struck out. Only once. Then Julien ran up behind him and stuck a syringe into the back of the Doppelgänger's neck. There was one last unearthly scream, and then the Doppelgänger passed out.

Panting, Don helped his mother out of her painful position—smashed through the dashboard window—just as soon as Julien had pulled the Doppelgänger's limp form away and dropped the seventeen-year-old killer on the street pavement. Seemingly back to her normal, practical self, Via dove into the back seat, hunting for something that could serve as temporary bandaging for Scarlet's knife wound.

Scarlet sat down heavily on the pavement, leaning weakly against the front of the car. She shut her eyes, knowing the weakness and pain would presently pass. Then a shadow fell across her face, and she looked up, her eyes flying open.

A helmeted, black-dressed figure stood there. Scarlet blinked a couple of times before she realized that it was her daughter, back in "Shadow" gear.

Via pushed up her visor, kneeling down to temporarily bandage her mother's bleeding shoulder. In the meantime, Don came back with a glass of water he'd managed to get his hands on. Julien went to talk to the police.

"Are you alright?" Via whispered, her eyes worried. "Is this helping or is it making it worse?"

Scarlet smiled vaguely as she took the water from her eldest son. "It's helping. Thank you."

She was happy about the victory they had just won, but even more happy to see Via's normal self again. It was such a relief.

"Mom." Via leaned close, concern flickering in her blue-purple eyes. "Mom, are you... Are you disappointed in me?"

Scarlet shook her head, ignoring the added pain it caused her. "Why would I be disappointed, Via Pacis Whyte? Tell me that," Scarlet went on as Via's eyes opened wide in honest happiness. "Why should I ever be disappointed? Because you didn't want to be strong? Listen, Via, strength means nothing to me. Absolutely nothing. What matters to me is that you don't think you're weak."

"But, Mom, I am..." The sentence trailed unfinished from Via's lips.

"You're not weak, Via," Scarlet insisted, reaching out with her good hand to gently remove the bloodstained helmet from her daughter's sweaty, scarred face. "You have a near-perfect body, a somehow unbroken mind, a traumatized memory, and yet, you're an angel at heart."

She pushed Via's bangs out of the twenty-year-old's eyes, looking into the blue-purple eyes Scarlet was so fond of. "You have a good heart, Via. You're a Trooper, you're a Whyte... You can love, you can live...and, Via, don't ever let anything change that. Because you mean the world to me."

Via was speechless. A single tear trickled down her scarred cheek, but Scarlet had one last thing to say.

"You've been broken again and again, butterfly. But now I want to see you spread your wings and fly."

THE END

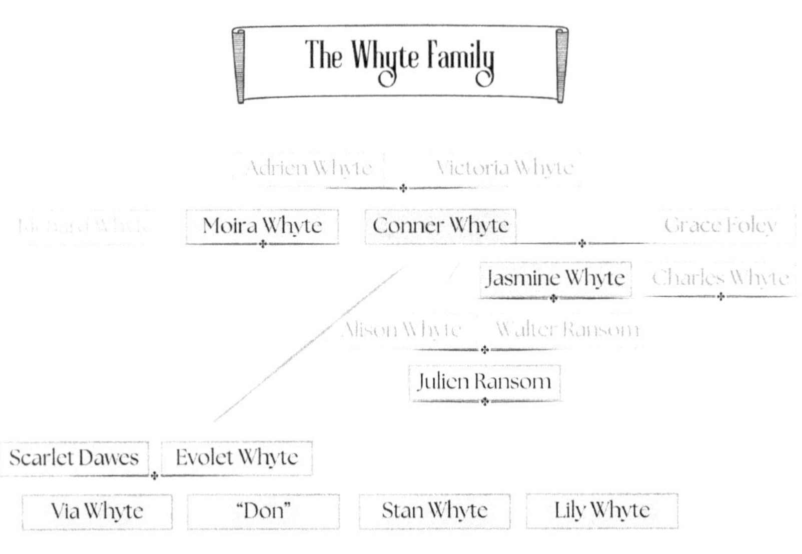

Glossary

Encephalon	Lyndon's HQ in A1
G-Fiber	a superhuman-proof cloth substance
Myelin	a chemical that freezes the blood stream
Paradraline	anti-adrenaline used to stabilize T6 in A3
Purple Crystal	a special substance that can cut G-Fiber
Schwann	the machine that maintained the uniforms in A1
Schwann2	the drug in A2 to wipe out those with T4
Schwann3	Eternyti's "cure" in A3
T4	superhuman serum (original)
T5	annotated superhuman serum (A2)
HT5	fully realized T5 (A2)
T6	HT5+T4, formulated on accident by Zaire (A2-A3)
T6S	T6 stabilizer formulated by Scarlet Dawes (A3)
T7	Generational T4+HT5 (first found in Via Whyte, A4)

Timeline (A)

2021

Richard Whyte is killed in a bank robbery.

2024

- Early Fall: Conner is kidnapped; T4 is tested and approved.

- 1 December: The Purple Blitzkrieg begins at 4:00 PM.

- That night: U.S. paratroopers are dropped into Annapolis.

- 8 December: Conner is rescued; reunion with Moira.

- 9 December: Final attack on Encephalon; American victory.

2026

Conner and Violet are married.

2027

Evolet is born; his parents flee to Iceland.

2041

- Early Fall: Evolet's family returns to the USA.

- Early December: Jasmine is kidnapped and rescued.

2042

- February: Twins' birthday; Riley Fletcher is killed.

- One week later: T4 prison inmates die silently.

- Two days later: Rocket's planned release; Victor climax.

- 9 June: Violet discovers a vial of T4 is missing.

Timeline (B)

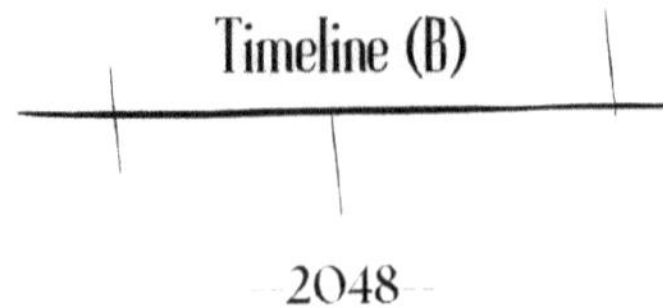

2048

Early school year: Evolet and Jasmine's covers at college are blown.

2049

- 1 May: Ayan Monet attacks the college during the graduation.

- 8 May: Jasmine and Evolet tangle with Ayan and Louis.

- 9 May: Civilians are killed; two children kidnapped.

- 10-11 May: More children are kidnapped. Leopard is killed; Conner is infected with T6.

- 14 May: Kidnappers and children leave Annapolis.

- 21 May: Whyte parents leave; the kids follow hours later.

- 24 May: Mountain fight; Conner, Violet, and Joyce hospitalized.

- 27 May: Ayan and Louis are conquered; Whyte parents are injected with Schwann3.

- 29 May: Evolet, Jasmine, and Michael escape Eternyti Labs.

- 3-4 June: Eternyti Labs is conquered; the Whytes arrive in Mexico City.

- 5 June (evening): Violet leaves.

- 6 June (morning): Moira leaves; Jasmine, Evolet, and Scarlet follow Violet.

- 9 June: The final battle; Violet dies.

- 16 June: Evolet reads Violet's letter.

2051

Summer: Conner realizes his T4 abilities are returning.

Timeline (C)

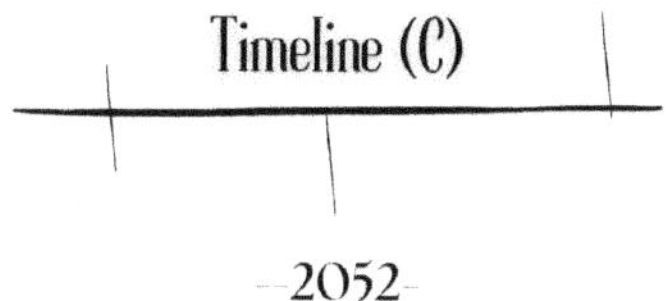

2052

- **6 January:** Whyte home is attacked; Evolet's family is torn apart; Via is taken.
- **August:** Don is born and taken from Scarlet.
- **Later in the year:** Concentration camp escape fails; most of the Whytes are killed.

2059

International computer crisis.

2067

- **18 April:** Jasmine is arrested; Julien discovers his heritage.

- **20 April:** Scarlet escapes.

- **21 April:** Walter Ransom is arrested.

- **22 April:** Julien confronts Eryka and meets Via.

- **23 April (morning):** Julien and Via see themselves denounced on TV.

- **23 April (night):** Wolf Pack is formalized; Via is scarred; Via and Julien find Jasmine; Eryka's war against WIPA begins.

- **24–25 April:** Reunion with Scarlet; Teresa Pervitto joins; Karol Lasek joins; the team departs to free prisoners in Antarctica.

- **30 April:** WIPA officials killed; Walter Ransom killed by Eryka; Superhuman Whytes save the day.

- **1 May:** Whytes return to the USA; Ceasefire the next evening.

- **3 May (evening):** Treaty is signed; Wolf escapes, nearly kills Via, and is struck by lightning.

- **Six weeks later:** Eryka is freed.

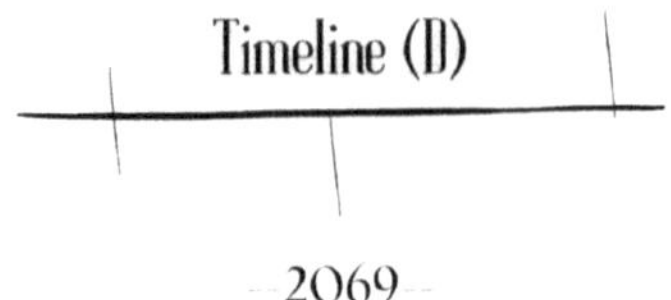

Timeline (II)

2069

- Christmas: Via is kidnapped.

- 27–28 December: Evolet and Scarlet confront Eryka in Australia. They return; the plane crashes.

- Simultaneously: Jasmine and Julien are kidnapped (along with younger Whytes).

2070

- Early January: Evolet, Scarlet, and Eryka are kidnapped.

- The next day: Eryka is killed; the Whytes are freed; Diana is defeated.

- Summer: Don Whyte is freed (in Germany).

- A couple of weeks later: German gang collapses internally; Don is independent.

2073

Don meets Julien Ransom and travels to the USA.

- One month later: Don meets Via and is returned to the Whyte family. Simultaneously, the Doppelgänger is released.

- One month later: Via is nearly killed by the Doppelgänger.

- One week later: Conner is attacked by the Doppelgänger; Scarlet resolves to stop the Doppelgänger.

- The next day: Scarlet meets Eris (defects).

- The following day: Whytes hunt the Doppelgänger; Eris is killed; the Doppelgänger is defeated.

About the Author

Gabrielle Marie Kozak is an American author whose fiction explores pressure, endurance, and the cost of refusing to surrender oneself to oppressive systems. Her debut, *The Trooper Series*, began as a body of work written before she graduated high school and introduced her recurring focus on individual sovereignty under strain.

The eldest of nine children, Gabrielle spent nearly two years as a religious sister before turning her attention fully to writing and publishing. Her stories center on those who carry responsibility, those who break beneath it, and those who survive when systems fail.

She lives in Nebraska and loves writing, coffee, and all things Poland.

Website: **gmariaek.com**

Also by Gabrielle Marie Kozak

Thank you for reading!

If this story stayed with you, I would be grateful if you'd consider leaving a short review. Reviews help books like this find the readers who need them.

Your time, your attention, and your support truly matter.

If you'd like to continue reading my work, **The Trooper Series** is the best place to start.

Trooper A1: The Purple Blitzkrieg is the first book in the series.

Trooper A1: The Purple Blitzkrieg

SHE LOST HER BROTHER - JUST NOT THE WAY SHE THOUGHT.

Moira Whyte refuses to believe the **bloody evidence** that confirms her brother's death. Instead, she begins to hack into **Encephalon**, the underground network built to **subjugate the entire world.**

She's right. Her brother isn't dead.

He's worse than dead.

Trooper A2: "Little Trooper"

HE WAS RAISED TO BE SAFE. HE WAS BORN TO BE SOMETHING ELSE.

When **Evolet Whyte** first meets his real parents and siblings, they **shatter** his view on life–forever. **His mother has a story.** Does he trust her–or does he believe what **history itself** tells him?

The **truth won't wait** for him to find it in the skyscrapers and the classrooms. It's coming to find him–and it could d**estroy** both Evolet and his new-found family.

To survive, Evolet must **discover and awaken** the "Little" Trooper within.